Incident at River Bend

When Steve Carrington, the sheriff of River Bend, saves a
young and desperate thief from a lynch mob, he is content to
send the kid packing with his life intact. However when a mysterious army sergeant arrives, fresh out of jail for armed
robbery, tension in the town builds.

Wesley Carradine is convinced the sergeant is sitting on a
pile of loot the authorities never found and sends his private
henchmen to investigate. All the while, however, with the help
of a company of bandits, Carradine is organizing a more
devious ploy that will really turn the town on its head.

Avarice, honour and the battle for supremacy fuel the saga
that ensues, as the actions of a greedy few take a grip on the
town.

Incident at River Bend

Lee Lejeune

A Black Horse Western

ROBERT HALE · LONDON

ISBN 978-0-7198-1305-4

Robert Hale Limited
Clerkenwell House
Clerkenwell Green
London EC1R 0HT

www.halebooks.com

Typeset by
Derek Doyle & Associates, Shaw Heath
Printed and bound in Great Britain by
CPI Antony Rowe, Chippenham and Eastbourne

CHAPTER ONE

Steve Carrington was eating his midday meal at the usual table in the River Bend Hotel. Though there were other folk in the saloon, nobody was sharing the table with him because they knew he preferred to eat alone except when Maria was around, which wasn't often at that time of day because she was too busy with her other customers.

Maria was the owner of the River Bend Hotel and she had built it up from practically nothing into the best hotel in the town of River Bend. Maria was tall and slender and everyone in River Bend regarded her very highly. She was a great businesswoman and she always gave a fair deal.

Now she was moving briskly behind the bar supervising her assistants and seeing to the needs of her customers, though she did pause a moment from time to time to give Steve a glance and he replied with a lopsided wink.

Steve was sheriff of River Bend. He'd been in the job for just over five years and was becoming a permanent fixture. Not that he spent too much time sitting in Maria's saloon eating his lunch. Being sheriff obviously involved duties such as locking up rowdies and subduing trouble makers in the town and Steve had something of a talent for that.

River Bend was a growing town and everyone was blossoming with it, including the criminal element. Steve had thought about swearing in a deputy but that wasn't easy since the pay wouldn't be enough to keep a mouse in cheese. A deputy needed to be reliable and, if push came to shove, good with a gun too. Steve had been brought up toting guns ever since he was half a knee high to a grasshopper. His father was a farmer with an acreage further up the river. Not much of a farm to support a growing family. Henry Carrington supplemented his living by hunting and fishing and occasional guiding, though there wasn't much call for that these days. He wasn't a good farmer but he had big ambitions for his sons. He had wanted Steve to go to college and become something important like a lawyer or a doctor, or maybe a veterinarian. But Steve was a bitter disappointment to Henry; now he was just the sheriff of a hick town and apparently with no ambition to be anything more.

True he had spent a couple of years in service during the late war but that was now in the past; it was time to settle down and become, well, civilized.

'Go, get yourself an education and make something of your life,' Henry had said to Steve. 'You have the brains. You want to be a no good farmer like me for the rest of your life?'

Though Steve could see the point and appreciated his father's ambition for him he just sat in the sheriff's office, biding his time while the world flowed all round him like water round a stone.

Having finished his meal, he was wiping his plate clean with a hunk of Maria's home cooked bread. He didn't want to waste any of that good gravy, did he? When he looked up he saw Maria grinning at him. To say grinning was something of an exaggeration; it was more of an appreciative smile. Maria's good nature and fine features forbade anything like a grin. They say you can read a person's character in her face and Maria had an open, friendly nature; she had a ready smile for everybody.

'So I see you enjoyed your chuck, Steve,' she said in the pleasant contralto voice that reflected her nature. When Sam, the pianist was around, she sometimes sang during the evening to entertain her customers and nobody had ever complained. On the contrary, she was usually greeted with wild cheers. At roundup time when the waddies came in to squander their pay they often joined in with a chorus of B flats and A majors! It was a lot more enthusiastic than tuneful.

When she commented on Steve's ability to appreciate his food he raised his crust and tilted it towards her. A man doesn't want to waste his gravy, does he? 'Just as good as always, though not quite as good as it used to be when you did all the cooking yourself, Maria.'

Maria was a nice name, he figured. Better than Mary. It had a good musical tone that always sent a shiver down his spine.

'Flattery won't get you far, Mr Carrington,' she said in that melodious tone.

'Well,' Steve retorted, 'it's got me pretty well along the road so far, didn't it?'

She was smiling again. 'You need to settle down and find yourself a good wife,' she said.

Steve moved his head from side to side and opened his hands in a fatalistic gesture. 'Who'd want a tumbleweed man of the law like me?' he asked. He screwed his mouth up in an expression if profound skepticism. 'Anyway, I don't think I'm the marrying kind. If I got myself hitched like an old cart horse to a rig, my pa and ma wouldn't stop

7

laughing and jeering from now till doomsday.'

Maria gave him an appraising stare. 'That's a fair long time, Steve, and I don't know if I'd agree with you on that. You're not bad looking . . . that is for a sheriff.'

Steve gave a hoarse laugh and then stopped. He was looking at Maria intently. 'How about you, Maria, would a fine woman like you take a man like me on?'

Maria paused and looked dubious. It wasn't the first time Steve had proposed to her. She had thought about it often. But he was right; after all, what could he offer? In a hotel like the River Bend you needed a man with dignity who commanded respect.

Steve had respect of a kind to be sure. The criminal element in River Bend, especially those who spent a little time in the town hoosegow, certainly respected him.

The difficulty with Steve was you could never be sure he was serious.

Maria had very little time to consider Steve's offer because, at that moment, there was a scuffle at the door and a man came tumbling in backwards. He collided with a table and landed with a thump on his back. He stretched out cold. It was Sam, the piano player and there was blood on his head.

'Oh, my God!' a woman gasped.

Everyone in the saloon stopped talking and turned. Maybe Sam was drunk which was unusual since Sam drank only whiskey and water in small doses.

Maria stepped back with her hand held to her mouth. She was no shrinking violet and had once knocked a man off a chair and on to his back with a single punch for insulting a friend. But this seemed serious! After all, Sam was a man of peace who would never squash a fly if he could avoid it.

Steve rose to his feet surprisingly quickly. He wiped his mouth on his red bandanna and thought of moving to assist his friend Sam. But just at that moment the cause of Sam's fall materialized in the form of a man with a yellow bandanna across his face and below the eyes, and he had a Colt revolver in his hand.

The man stood for a moment and then raised the gun. There was a huge echoing bang as he fired a shot at the ceiling. 'OK,' he said. 'Nobody makes a move, nobody gets hurt!'

People stared at the man agog. There hadn't been a hold up in River Bend in recent memory. Was this a joke of some kind? Nobody knew how to react.

Then Maria made a move towards the interloper as though she meant to try to stop him, but Steve grabbed her by the arm to restrain her.

The man was looking directly at Maria.

'Now you just take out your dollars and gold watches and put them in this hat,' he said hoarsely. 'Then I'll leave you all in peace.'

This guy must be desperate and he's as nervous as a cat, Steve thought. He knew from experience that a nervous man can be somewhat unpredictable.

He moved from behind the table and took a single step towards the man.

'Don't move!' the man shouted. 'You want to get yourself killed, sheriff?'

Steve paused. 'You want blood on your hands?' he asked, keeping his voice calm and low.

'There ain't gonna be no blood,' the man replied. 'Not if you do what I told you. Money, that's what I need. I just said it, didn't I?' He sounded somewhat peevish as well as aggressive as though he was surprised that nobody took him

9

seriously, despite the gun.

'Then what?' Steve said. 'You think you can ride out of here in one piece after you've taken the money?'

The man's eyes darted this way and that and eventually fell on Maria again. 'You the owner of this dump?' he asked belligerently.

Maria gave a slight nod. 'Sure I'm the owner but it's not a dump. You just blew a hole in my ceiling.'

Maria has plenty of sand in her craw, Steve thought. But this is a matter for me. He took a step to one side so that he was standing between Maria and the masked man. 'Let me tell you something, Mister Nobody in the River Bend Hotel is going to give you any dollars or gold watches. So why don't you just drop that gun before it goes off again and kills someone. Then we can talk sense.'

That caused a murmur of approval among the customers in the saloon but the man tossed his head and seemed to stiffen.

Steve was beginning to feel a little concerned. Though the saloon was by no means full there were one or two rough and determined characters drinking at the bar and he knew that at least one of them would be armed. Though Maria had a no gun policy in the hotel there were one or two exceptions such as Steve himself. If one of those more aggressive characters like Brig Bailey took a chance and pulled a gun, all hell mighty break loose.

'OK,' Brig suddenly piped up. 'I'll throw in a greenback or two. Then you can ride out with your head held high.' He slid off his stool and took a step or two towards the robber with a dollar bill in his hand. Brig was a tall, thickset man with a curly moustache. He owned a thriving hardware business in town and was thought to be quite rich though notoriously mean. So, when he held out the dollar bill

10

everyone laughed.

Steve could see that the would-be robber was becoming more agitated. His hand was shaking and he might easily have fired another shot without intending to.

Now Sam, the pianist, was beginning to groan. He opened his eyes and raised his head and looked at his assailant and, in that second the would-be robber's attention was diverted.

It was long enough for Steve to draw his single action Colt and cock it.

The robber swung towards him and fired off a round.

There was a gasp and a scream but the shot passed harmlessly between Steve and Brig Bailey and embedded itself in the wall, fortunately missing everyone on the way.

Though big and burly Brig Bailey wasn't slow moving, he swung his meaty fist and felled the assailant with a single blow. The robber dropped on to his back and lay spread-eagled, staring up at the ceiling. The next instant he was staring along the barrel of Steve's single-action Colt.

Brig Bailey reached down and hauled the would-be robber to his feet as if he were no more than a sack of potatoes. Steve retrieved the pistol and stuck it through his gunbelt. Maria was close by, tutting and shaking her head.

Now everyone in the saloon laughed with relief.

'What do we do with him?' Brig Bailey asked, giving the would-be robber a shove in the ribs.

'Why don't we string him up to one of Maria's beams and let him dangle,' someone suggested.

'Just like one of those dead pigs you got hanging in your store,' another man responded.

'We don't want to insult the hotel with his presence, do we?' Brig Bailey shouted. 'I figure we should just haul him outside and hang him up at the street corner outside the undertaker's store. It could be a good advertising sign for the undertaking business.'

Everybody was crowding in on the intended victim and he began to look more like a whipped cur than a man.

Some of the sensitive customers were more interested in poor Sam than the would-be robber. Maria and one or two other women were helping him up and examining his wound which was still bleeding.

'We must get you to Doc MacFadden,' Maria was saying. 'That's a nasty gash on your head.'

Poor Sam had momentarily lost consciousness after the fall and he was staggering around only half aware of the proceedings.

Steve was looking at the would-be robber and saw that he was little more than a bag of bones. His eyes had a strange pleading look about them. 'You gonna let them kill me?' he said to Steve.

'You bet we're going to kill you,' Brig Bailey said, giving him a hefty punch in the ribs. 'If you do a hold-up and threaten to kill people what else can you expect? "Tooth for tooth and eye for an eye,"' he quoted.

That gave rise to a series of jeers and hoots of approval from the customers.

Steve figured things were getting pretty serious. He looked at Maria and she shook her head. 'Now, back off,' he said to the assembled guests. 'There's gonna be no killing right now.'

'What d'you aim to do?' Brig Bailey asked bluntly.

'What I'm gonna do is to take the man down to the jail and lock him in a cell for his own good. If you act before you think it can lead to bad consequences. When bad consequences are fatal it's too late to regret your decision.'

Steve wasn't exactly a gifted speaker; so when he did say

something, folk tended to listen. After all, he was the sheriff, wasn't he? People started shaking their heads and growling in agreement or approval according to their judgement.

Steve struck his gun in the would-be robber's ribs and edged him towards the door. The man walked quite briskly ahead as though he was relieved to be out of the hotel.

'Thanks, sheriff,' he said out of the corner of his mouth.

'Thanks for what?' Steve grunted, pushing him along more firmly.

'Thanks for saving my life,' the would-be robber said, slightly out of breath.

'Don't speak too soon,' Steve replied somewhat tartly. 'If you'd killed someone in there you'd be kicking your legs in the air by now. Folks here don't care to have their meals spoiled like that.'

The sheriff's office and jail was no more than a hundred yards down the street and they made sprightly progress, urged on by a crowd of yapping dogs and children and a few men and women who had come out of the hotel to follow them.

As they moved along the sidewalk, Steve was thinking to himself: That was a damned fool thing to do, holding up a saloon at gunpoint while folks were busy drinking and eating their meals. No more chance than a snowball in hell!

In fact, he thought, it was like some kind of suicide mission. The man walking ahead of him was like an amateur playing at being a hold-up man. He was no more than a callow boy with no more than a few hairs sprouting from his chin.

When they reached the office Steve turned at the door. 'OK, folks, the show's over. You can take yourselves off and get about your business. There's no more to see. And take

INCIDENT AT RIVER BEND

those mangy dogs with you, too. I don't want them hanging around making the place untidy.'

Someone chuckled. The sheriff would have his little joke.

Steve opened the door of one of the cells and ushered the would-be robber inside with a slight bow, saying, 'Be my guest.'

The would-be robber shambled inside, looking somewhat relieved. 'What happens now?' he asked.

Steve stroked his chin. 'That, my friend, rather depends on the circumstances.'

The young man, who was in fact no more than a raw youth, sat down on the cot and pondered. 'What circumstances?' he asked after a second.

Steve nodded. 'The circumstances of you firing off three shots in a respectable hotel and trying to extort money with the help of a gun. People don't care for that sort of thing in these parts and neither does the law.'

The young lawbreaker sat back and pondered for a moment longer. Steve looked at him steadily and saw he had the appearance of someone who had never eaten adequately before.

'When was your last meal?' he asked the youth.

'Can't remember,' the youth replied. 'Some time yesterday, probably.'

'Well,' said Steve. 'You keep civilized and I'll send down to the River Bend and ask them to bring in something. Holding up hotels must give you an appetite and we can't have you starving before they hang you, can we?'

The lawbreaker blinked a couple of times. 'Thanks, Sheriff,' he said quietly.

Steve had produced a small notebook and a stub of pencil. 'Now I have to ask you a few questions and it might help if you give me straight answers.'

'I'll do that, Sheriff,' the youth answered in a humble tone.

There were two cots in the cell; the youth was sitting on the left and Steve was sitting across from him on the right. The door was open but Steve wasn't unduly worried.

'Name?' he said.

'Eleazer Stebbins,' the youth replied.

Steve looked up briefly and wrote down the name. 'Is that an e a?' he asked.

'Sure, Eleazer Stebbins.'

'Now old are you, Eleazer?'

'Eighteen,' the youth replied.

Steve wrote down the number eighteen.

'That's a bit young to take up robbing and killing,' he said. 'Have you thought about that, Eleazer?'

A sly grin appeared on the young man's face. Then he frowned. 'Well, it's like this, sir. I didn't rightly know what to do. I weren't no good around the farm. My stepdad beat up on me. So I decided to cut loose and split.'

'So you've got nowhere to go, Eleazer Stebbins,' Steve said. In fact he had begun to empathize with this hold-up youth who had been bullied by his stepfather. 'Well, now,' he added, 'I expect the circuit judge in around a week's time and he'll have to decide what to do with you.'

Steve locked the door of the cell and went out into the adjoining office where there was a pinewood desk and a shelf with a few books, mostly about the law. Steve sometimes consulted the law books but he was by no means an expert. He just followed his instincts about what was right and just and good for River Bend – like Judge Bean of Texas fame, only Bean wasn't really a properly elected judge and he often had offenders hanged without just cause.

15

Steve was worried about Eleazer Stebbins. Keeping him fed in the town jail for a week wouldn't be popular and, sooner or later, there would be a fuss.

The fuss started sooner than he had expected. Towards sundown, as he sat behind his desk, pondering over the future, someone pushed open the office door and came in. It was a sharp featured man with a small pointed beard. He wore a long black coat and a black hat that made him look about six feet, two.

'Ah, Mr Mayor,' Steve said as he uncurled himself from behind his desk.

'Sheriff Carrington,' the mayor said in a formal tone. 'They tell me you've had a problem today.'

'Sure, there was a slight difficulty,' Steve conceded. 'I've got the offender locked up in the jail here.'

'Well, that's both good and bad,' the mayor said cryptically.

'Good and bad.' Steve turned the words over in his mind. 'How good and how bad?'

'Good as much as the malefactor is locked up,' the mayor said. 'Bad because some of the citizens want to take him out and hang him by the neck at the corner of the block.'

Steve sat back in his chair. 'Well, they can't do that, Mr Mayor. You know that and I know that and I can't allow that to happen.'

'On whose authority?' the mayor asked sharply.

'On the authority of the law.' Steve tapped the badge of office on his chest.

Mayor Shapley, a prominent member of the business community in the town, paused to consider matters. He wasn't used to being contradicted by anyone. Yet he had respect for the sheriff.

'As it happens, I agree with you,' he said after a moment. 'But consider this, Mr Carrington. You can't guard the prisoner all day and all night. If the citizens want the prisoner dead, sooner or later they're going to come right in here and take him out and hang him.'

'You've got a point there, Mr Mayor. That's why I'm gonna ask you to assist me.'

Mayor Shapley stiffened slightly. 'How would that be, Mr Carrington?'

Steve drummed on the desk with his fingers. 'If you agree to taking turns with me to guard the prisoner through the night, come sun-up the world will look a whole lot brighter and those would-be hangmen will begin to see sense and go about their legitimate business.'

A brief smile flickered across the mayor's lean face. Before he had gone into business some years earlier he had been a bit of a hell raiser himself and he liked a challenge.

'Very well, Mr Carrington,' he said. 'I believe we've got a deal here. I'll go home now and sleep awhile. Come midnight I'll walk over and sit outside on the porch while you take your rest.'

'That's a good deal,' Steve said. He stood up and the two shook hands.

A little later someone else appeared at the door: Maria and one of her serving girls carrying a covered tray.

'Is everything at peace here?' Maria asked. 'We brought a little chow for the prisoner.'

'He'll be glad of that. I can hear his belly rumbling from here already. It'll be the first good meal he's had since he took in his mother's milk.'

The serving girl, whose name was Emily, gave Steve a bashful smile. She was no more than fifteen but she had always dreamed of Steve as a potential lover. 'Should I take it to him now?' she asked.

Steve had been playing a game of patience and he was glad of the interruption. He hauled himself up from his desk, took the keys and unlocked the cell door. The prisoner, Eleazer Stebbins, was lying on his bed staring up at the ceiling, but when he smelled food approaching, he turned and rose cautiously to his feet. 'Is this for me?' he asked suspiciously.

'This is your lucky hour,' Steve told him.

Maria stood outside the cell watching and she saw how Eleazer Stebbins fell on his food and devoured it. 'That boy's half starved,' she said to Steve quietly.

'Which explains a lot,' Steve agreed.

'You know they want to hang him,' she said. 'I heard Brig Bailey and some of the others talking. I think they're planning something.'

'How's Sam?' Steve asked her.

'He's recovering. The doc looked him over and he'll be fine. He'll soon be playing the piano good as new.'

'Sooner the better,' Steve said. 'The more he plays, the less folk will be inclined towards violence.'

'Well, I do hope you're right,' Maria said.

CHAPTER TWO

After the tray had been removed – and there wasn't much more than a smear of gravy left on the plate – the prisoner perked up considerably.

'You know, Sheriff, that was the best meal I've had in a century.'

'A century's a good long time,' Steve said, 'but I'm glad you enjoyed it because, if those walking whiskey vats get their way, it might be your last meal.'

The boy shivered slightly. 'I shouldn't have done it, Sheriff. I know that, but I was desperate.'

Steve grinned. 'It wasn't so much what you did,' he said. 'It was the way you did it. If you hadn't got close to killing someone I'd have said that was the most bungled attempt at robbery I've ever seen.'

'Tell me,' said the youth. 'That man I knocked over. Is he gonna be all right?'

'I hear he's recovering,' Steve replied. 'Probably got a pretty sore head, that's all.'

'What about my horse?' Eleazer Stebbins asked him.

'You don't need to worry none about your mare,' Steve assured him. 'She's in the livery stable right now, feeding up on the best hay available. Her future looks a lot better than yours right now.'

Steve was right about 'the walking whiskey vats'. As he spoke to the prisoner he heard shouts from the sidewalk, followed by the noise of fists banging at the door. 'I think trouble's coming knocking,' he said. 'I suggest you curl up under your blanket and pretend to be asleep while I go out and attend to business.'

He took down his gunbelt and checked his gun. Then he took down a Winchester and checked that. He went to the door.

'Did someone come a'knocking?' he enquired.

He opened the door and looked out. Steve wasn't easily surprised but seeing at least a dozen men, some of them on horseback, spread out along the main drag, did give him pause for thought.

Brig Bailey was on the sidewalk with a revolver tucked into his belt and he was obviously taking the initiative in this matter.

'Is there something I can do for you, gentlemen?' Steve asked benignly.

'Sure is,' Brig Bailey said. 'You can open that damned cell door and bring the prisoner out to face his just desserts.'

The men spread out behind him gave a chorus of grunts and approving jeers.

'We've taken a vote on it and that's our unanimous decision,' Brig Bailey announced.

Steve raised his eyebrows and appeared to consider matters. 'Unanimous decision. Well, that's really something, Brig. Only one problem, though.'

'And what's that?' Brig Bailey enquired gruffly.

'That's because I'm holding the prisoner until the judge gets in next week. Then there'll be a legitimate trial and the

20

prisoner will be sentenced according to the law.'

'That's all hogwash.' Brig Bailey turned to his followers for support and there was a slight stirring among them. Whether with approval or disapproval, Steve couldn't be sure.

'That isn't hogwash, Brig. That's the law and I'm here to make it stick.'

Brig's hand moved to the revolver stuffed into his belt. 'Well, law or no law, we're coming in to take that boy out and make him swing.'

Steve was standing with the Winchester across his body. In order to cover Brig Bailey he would need to swing it out towards him. Before he could do that, Brig Bailey could yank the Colt from his belt and fire off a round. It wasn't likely but it was possible.

'Listen, Brig, I understand your concern but I can't let you do that.'

Brig Bailey stared at him for a moment and then took half a step forward and it was in that second that Steve made his move. He kicked out at the man's legs and brought the Winchester round in an arc to make contact with his midriff.

Brig Bailey staggered back and pulled his gun.

Steve stepped in quickly and raised the Winchester. He struck Brig Bailey on the chest and the big man staggered back and pitched off the sidewalk. As he fell, he fired his revolver; the round might have hit Steve, it was that close.

There was a gasp from the onlookers and then a tense silence. Would they surge forward or back off? Would Steve fall or stagger back wounded?

Steve swung the Winchester and held it low. Brig Bailey was by no means finished. His pride had been punctured and he might still do something foolish.

'Now why don't you boys go home and rest,' Steve sang out, 'before we have a tragedy on our hands?'

There was a stirring among the men as though they didn't know which way to go.

Then another voice was heard. 'The sheriff's right. Go home and take your rest. We don't want things to get out of hand here, do we?'

Everyone turned to see the mayor sitting on his black horse.

'Many thanks for your support,' Steve said after the would-be necktie party had dispersed.

Mayor Shapley gave his usual half-approving smile. 'Heard the commotion. Thought I ought to come and lend a hand. Now, why don't you turn in for a bit of shut eye and I'll take the next watch.'

'I think I'll just do that, Mr Mayor.'

However, instead of retiring to his room behind the sheriff's office, he walked along the sidewalk to the River Bend Hotel. The lights were on but there was a sign up outside that said closed. So Steve went to the side door and gave his usual secret knock: three short taps and, after a pause, two more taps in quick succession. After a few moments Maria peered cautiously out of the door. When she saw him she pushed open the door and beckoned him in.

Steve went into the now empty saloon and sat down at his usual table. 'Any chance of a drink?' he said. 'I can sure use one.'

Maria went behind the bar and poured a measure of her best whiskey. She brought it to his table on a tray and set it down before him.

'I saw what you did out there,' she said. 'That boy's lucky to be alive.' She had seen how Steve had knocked Brig

22

Bailey back off the sidewalk with the butt of his Winchester and she had experienced a surge of pride in him. Unbeknown to Steve she had been standing under the ramada of the general store no more than a few yards away and she had her own Colt in her hand. She would have used it too, if necessary. Maria was that sort of woman.

'What's with the boy now?' she asked.

'Sleeping like a new born babe,' Steve said. He sipped the best whiskey and sighed. 'That tastes good,' he said. He told her how Mayor Shapley was standing guard.

'He's a good man,' she said. 'He might be a little strange sometimes, but he knows his duty. What will happen to that boy?'

'Lucky he didn't kill anybody,' Steve said. He told her how the judge would be riding in in a few days and, maybe, the matter would be settled. 'Don't feed that boy up too much or he might decide he wants to stay in jail. I don't know the full story but it looks like he's been starved for about eighteen years! And how's Sam?' he added.

'Sam's doing OK,' she said. 'Clara came to take him home after the doc had patched him up. After a good night's sleep he'll be back playing for his supper like before.'

'All's well that ends well,' Steve said. His eye fell on a copy of the county news sheet as he spoke. He read of a hold up man called Pete Pollinger who had just been released from jail. Not thought to be dangerous, he read beneath a grainy picture of the ex-convict. Then suddenly he sat right up. 'My God!' he said.

'What's that?' Maria said.

Steve placed his finger on the grainy photo. 'Why that's Pete Pollinger,' he said. 'I know that man.'

*

23

The country judge wired through to inform Steve that his schedule was running early and that he'd be in town in two days' time.

When Steve informed the prisoner, Eleazer Stebbins looked both alarmed and then relieved. 'What's going to happen to me?' he asked.

'That's for the judge to decide,' Steve said. 'The judge is wise in the law and he'll listen to both sides and whatever he decides that will be it.'

Steve and Eleazer Stebbins had been playing cards together in the cell. In the last two days Stebbins had eaten more than he had in years and it showed. His cheeks had started to glow with health and he looked as though he had put on several pounds. Much to his amazement Steve had decided that he was actually beginning to warm to the kid.

'I don't think you were made to be a desperado,' he said to Eleazer as he was dealing the cards one day. 'Killing people isn't your style,' he added.

Eleazer Stebbins looked down at the floor and blushed. 'Tell you the truth, sheriff, I don't think I could have carried it through.'

Next day just before noon Judge Mann arrived. He had ridden in on horseback from High Rock some twenty miles away. Judge Mann was a large rotund man who obviously liked his food. He had an ample belly and a long Christmassy beard which made him look like a benign old owl. When he was in town, he liked to stay at The River Bend Hotel because he enjoyed the hospitality there – especially the culinary delights Maria provided!

Mayor Shapley and he were old buddies. So the first thing the judge did was to dismount from his horse and call in on the mayor.

'Now then,' he said as the two of them met. 'You sent me a wire about that unfortunate would-be killer who hasn't got the sense he was born with.'

Mayor Shapley agreed that the attempted robbery had been just about as inept as a robbery could get. 'That boy must have been just plumb loco. Lucky he didn't kill anybody at the time.'

Judge Mann nodded sagely. 'Well, Bill, it's real good to see you. I think I'll go across and check in at Maria's place. She always does me proud, as you know.'

'That young woman is a credit to the town,' Mayor Shapley acknowledged.

Judge Mann walked across to the hotel to greet Maria who was expecting him. 'Well, Maria, you're looking just as beautiful as ever,' he said. 'If you were any other woman I'd expect to see you still shaking from that attempted robbery.'

Maria didn't bother to acknowledge the compliment. She knew that Judge Mann was somewhat prejudiced in his judgement of women, though he was a good man at heart.

'I hope you can provide me with my usual room,' he said, 'and, of course, I shall take my meals with you.'

'We shall be honoured, Judge,' Maria said. She knew the judge was married and had met his wife, a quiet and somewhat reserved woman who scarcely said a word in her husband's presence.

'Now, if you can spare me a little time,' the judge said, 'I should be obliged if you could give me an account of what happened on that fateful day.'

Maria sat down opposite the judge and gave him her version of the attempted robbery.

'So he didn't actually get to stealing anything?'

'Not a single dollar,' she said.

'That's good,' the judge said. 'That's very good. It seems

that Sheriff Carrington knows his business. He's a good man, Maria, a very good man.' He took out a silver cigar case and produced a rather fat cigar. 'I shall set up my court as usual in your back room. Can you arrange that, Maria?'

'Of course, sir. That private room is at your disposal.' It would be good for business, of course. Everyone who crowded into the room would need to be fed, especially the witnesses.

'Good, good, Maria. Shall we make it ten a.m. or maybe eleven. We don't want to hurry our breakfast, do we?'

'No, sir.'

'Good, good.' The judge wagged his head. 'I guess you've been feeding the prisoner up like the Christmas goose. How does he seem?'

Maria gave her description of Eleazer Stebbins. 'He's no more than a half starved boy,' she said.

'Well . . .' Judge Mann gave a judicious nod. 'That killer in New Mexico was no more than a boy. What was his name? William Bonney, I believe, and he had killed at least twenty men before he was eventually shot down. You can't go by looks. We have to remember that, Maria.'

Judge Mann walked the short distance to the sheriff's office where Steve Carrington was expecting him.

'Good day to you, Sheriff,' the judge said and the two men shook hands.

'What have you got for me?' Judge Mann asked.

Steve gave his account: two men up for starting a brawl, one for a drunken assault, and the Eleazer Stebbins case for attempted robbery with violence, of course.

The judge nodded and took a mental note. 'I came all this way for just that,' he said with apparent satisfaction. 'Good job I like this town so much.' He told Steve he'd be holding court in the hotel next morning at eleven.

'Before I go,' he said, 'I'll just take a peep at this young robber.' He peered round the door and saw Eleazer Stebbins scribbling something on a pad in his cell. Stebbins looked up and gave him a nervous nod. 'Looks like a frightened polecat,' the judge said to Steve. 'By the way, there's something I wanted to tell you.'

Steve Carrington pricked up his ears. 'What was that, Judge?'

'I've received news of a convict just released from the county penitentiary. A man called Pete Pollinger.'

'I know about that,' Steve said. 'I saw it in a newssheet in Maria's place. In fact, I knew the man way back.'

'How come?' the judge asked.

'We served together in the recent war. Pete Pollinger was my sergeant. He was a good buddy.'

'Well,' the judge said. 'It seems Mr Pollinger went to the bad after that. He robbed a few banks and ended up in gaol.'

'Did he kill anyone?' Steve asked.

'I don't think so,' the judge said. 'But he made a lot of enemies on the way. I thought I should mention it because the penitentiary isn't too far from here.' He looked at Steve with a twinkle in his eye. 'And as far as I know this guy Pollinger doesn't have too many friends.'

'Thanks for the warning, Judge,' Steve said.

Everyone knew Judge Mann and most thought he was a good and honourable guy who loved life but took his duties seriously. He weighed up the evidence as though with a pair of scales and usually came up with the right decision. He could be harsh in his judgement, but he could also be lenient, according to the evidence. Most of his cases had to do with livestock issues and the cattlemen generally bowed to his judgement.

At eleven o'clock next morning, in the courtroom at the rear of the hotel, the judgement chair was set up on a small dais facing the audience. Though the judge had quite a flair for theatricals, he didn't approve of words like 'audience'. He always referred to the people who attended as 'the public' and the public had every right to attend a trial in a democratic country. Judge Mann had high hopes for the people of the Western plains.

On this occasion the public area was almost full. People had crowded in from the saloon to see the prisoner and to hear what the judge would say. Maria was there, of course, and Sam, the piano player was sitting in the front row with Brig Bailey ready to give evidence. Sam was wearing his usual raffish style of clothes, a somewhat swanky check jacket and colourful cravat. Brig Bailey wore a dark suit and a dark necktie that he thought was more suitable for the occasion.

'Be upstanding for the judge,' one of Maria's waiters shouted.

The people all shuffled to their feet as the judge appeared through a back door. Judge Mann flapped his hand and sat down. 'Be seated, gentlemen, and ladies too,' he said with a benign smile. 'Let's get this session off the ground.'

First he dealt with the two brawlers and then the man accused of drunken assault. The brawlers said they couldn't remember much about what had happened. They were, in fact, buddies who had fallen out about some unnamed calico queen. The judge gave each a modest fine and sent them on their way as long as they promised to keep the peace in the future. The two brawlers seemed well satisfied.

Then came the older man who was accused of drunken assault. He claimed that the man he had assaulted had bad-mouthed his wife. The man he had assaulted claimed that it was all a misunderstanding and that the man accused had busted his lip and left him with a permanent headache and a shortage of teeth.

'Is that the truth?' said the judge. 'Please point to where it hurts.'

'What?' the supposed victim said. 'Why, sir, it hurts right here.' He pointed to his mouth and then to the back of his head.

'Does it hurt all the time?' the judge asked.

'Most of the time,' the man said. 'But more when I cough and shake my head.'

For some reason everyone in the courtroom laughed. The judge gave each man a fine for wasting the court's time.

Next came the most serious crime, the case of Eleazer Stebbins.

'Give the court your name,' the judge intoned solemnly.

Eleazer Stebbins gave his name in a quite humble-sounding tone.

'You are accused of trying to steal money and watches from the public in this hotel with the aid of a firearm. Do you plead guilty or not guilty to these charges?'

'Guilty,' Stebbins said without hesitation. 'But I didn't mean to kill nobody,' he added.

'Well, that's for the court to decide,' the judge said.

Then, despite the fact that the accused had pleaded guilty, Judge Mann decided to listen to the evidence and he called Maria, Sam the pianist, Brig Bailey and several others, including Steve Carrington. All gave similar accounts except that Brig Bailey's was more colourful than the rest. When he gave his account several of the rowdies who had wanted

Stebbins to hang gave an encouraging cheer.

Judge Mann held up his hand and, when the rowdies had calmed down, he gave his judgment. 'This man, who isn't much more than a boy, has admitted his guilt and I now need to pronounce the sentence.' He turned to face the guilty youth. 'I'm not going to sentence you to hard labour. We want good men in this county. So what I'm going to do is to place you in the hands of Father Sylvester here. . . .'

All eyes turned to the man in black habit standing at the back of the court.

'Father Sylvester has spoken to the prisoner and has agreed to take him under his wing. Eleazer Stebbins, you will remain at the Jesuit house under Father Sylvester's care until this time next year. You will work for the monks until you have served your term. I will then review the case and, if you have shown yourself to be repentant, you will be released.' He turned to scrutinize the prisoner. 'Do you understand, Eleazer Stebbins?'

Stebbins bowed his head. 'I understand, sir.'

'And if you overstep the mark in any way, you will be sent to the state penitentiary for as a long as I decree. Is that understood, Mr Stebbins?'

'Yes, sir.' The prisoner smiled faintly.

That was the end of the proceedings. Later that day Eleazer Stebbins rode out in the custody of three monks and Father Sylvester. Some of the witnesses were pleased. They figured the Jesuits were hard task masters and Stebbins wouldn't have an easy time. Others, including Brig Bailey, were still of the opinion that he should have been hanged. After all, when a man has swung he isn't likely to give you much more trouble, is he? That's what Brig Bailey said in Maria's hearing later.

After the trial the judge went off to have a long powwow with his buddy the mayor. Next morning, he would ride home to his wife. Though he was a benign character he bluntly refused to discuss the case with anyone but the mayor.

Steve was sitting at table with Maria that same evening. They were eating a well-deserved meal together.

'I'm glad we managed to save that boy,' Maria said. 'Brig Bailey and those other no-brain mule heads would have enjoyed seeing him swing but thanks to you he's still alive.'

'He won't have it easy up at the Jesuit House,' Steve said. 'That Father Sylvester is no easy touch. I shall look in from time to time and see how the boy's behaving.' He looked down and saw that Maria was holding a newssheet. 'What's that you've got there?' he asked her.

Maria unfolded the newssheet and spread it on the table. 'That's the paper we were looking at the other day. You remember? It was Pete Pollinger; you said you knew him.'

Steve looked down at the grainy face. 'Sure I knew him. We fought together in the recent war. The judge mentioned he's just been released from the county penitentiary.'

Maria looked at him and nodded. She had a strange feeling in her bones and it made her shiver.

When Steve looked up he saw the burly figure of Brig Bailey standing by the table. 'You know something,' Bailey said.

'I know a few things,' Steve said. 'Which particular thing had you in mind?'

'That kid should have swung for what he did.'

'Well, that's your opinion, Brig,' Steve said. 'But I'm afraid Judge Mann didn't agree with you.'

Brig Bailey took a step forward. 'And another thing,

Carrington. That butt you gave me with your Winchester. I didn't take kindly to that.'

'Well,' Steve reflected, 'that was all in the line of duty, Brig. I hope you don't harbour hard feelings about that.' Steve held out his hand.

Brig Bailey glared at him for a moment and then turned away.

'I don't think you made a friend there,' Maria said.

CHAPTER THREE

The arrival of the Wells Fargo stagecoach was always an event in River Bend and everyone who wasn't occupied would assemble outside the Wells Fargo office to watch the passengers disembark. They were usually a motley group: sewing machine salesmen, men and women looking for work in the town, and chancers who were ready to seize anything they could lay their hands on.

Steve Carrington went down to the Wells Fargo office to check out the passengers when he wasn't too busy with petty criminals in the town, and three weeks after the attempted robbery he was in the Wells Fargo office, talking to the agent Frederick Yango just before the coach from Big Rock was due in.

'How you doing, Fred?' he said.

Frederick Yango was a rather stout man with a fancy vest and a gold time piece and a chain stretched across his chest. On this occasion he took the watch from his pocket and consulted it with the aid of his rather minute spectacles. 'I'm doing just fine,' he said, 'but I'd be doing a whole lot better if I could see through these damned eye pieces.'

Though he complained, he was generally a good-natured man who enjoyed chatting. Of course, taking care of the stage wasn't a full time job. So he had a number of lucrative sidelines like running a small store which provided everything under the sun from coloured wool to Chinese sunshades. When he was in the Wells Fargo office his wife Melanie took care of the store.

'Expecting anyone in particular?' Steve asked casually.

'Just the usual bunch,' Yango said. 'They drift in and then drift out again. No big news in that.' He chuckled engagingly. 'You expecting anyone yourself?'

Steve grinned. 'I take them as they come, Fred. The good and the bad and the indifferent. In my line of business you don't ask too many questions. You have to be ready for anything that comes along.'

'That's a wise policy,' Yango said. 'I like to think I'm that way myself.' He peered at his gold timepiece a little more closely. 'She should be due any minute now.' He paused. 'By the way, I did hear something that might be of interest to you, Steve.'

Steve nodded. He knew that Yango kept his ear pretty close to the ground and, if there was something interesting happening, he would smell it from several miles off.

'You ever hear of a man called Pete Pollinger?' Yango said.

'I heard of him, sure,' Steve replied.

'Well, he got out of the county gaol just a few weeks back and a certain friend of mine – guy who lives in High Rock – sent me a wire through. Just a rumour but it might be true. According to my amigo, this ex-gaol bird might be headed our way.'

As they were speaking there was a great clatter and a haranguing as the stage coach pulled up outside. The run from High Rock was quite popular. At that time it was the only means of transport. It was drawn by a team of four horses and carried no fewer than a dozen passengers and their luggage. As well as a driver it carried a man with a shotgun to guard against hold-ups.

As Steve looked out the driver flourished his hat and gave a whoop. The man with the shotgun started hurling down the baggage, and Fred Yango went out to greet the passengers and help the ladies off the coach. One of the ladies was quite young – no more than eighteen – and the other, a middle-aged woman, was obviously her escort.

Steve watched as relations and friends greeted the new arrivals. The last to step off the coach was a tall thin man dressed in black and carrying no more than a small brown valise. The man stood on the sidewalk and looked about him as though he didn't know which way to go. Either there was nobody to meet him or they had failed to turn up.

He then took off his black Stetson and dragged a ker-chief across his brow. Clearly he had been sweating profusely.

As soon as the man took off his hat, Steve recognized him as Pete Pollinger.

Their eyes met and Pete Pollinger looked relieved.

Steve stepped forward and offered his hand.

'It's been a long time, Steve,' Pollinger said in a strangely cracked tone.

'A long time,' Steve replied.

'I've been in gaol,' Polllinger admitted without undue ceremony.

'Yes, I heard that.'

'I just got out,' Pollinger said.

'I heard that too.'

Pollinger took a rag out of his pocket, turned his face away, and began to cough. It was a deep rattling cough and Pollinger spat something into the rag.

'Are you sick?' Steve asked him.

'No, I'm not sick, I'm dying,' Pollinger said in a matter-of-fact tone. 'I couldn't stay in the gaol any longer because they have no hospital facilities. So, when your sentence is up they just kick you out on your arse into the wide world.' He gave a sheepish, half-apologetic grin.

Steve suddenly caught a glimpse of the past when he and Pete Pollinger were in the Northern army together. Pete Pollinger had been a very efficient soldier at that time – a man you could rely on in an emergency, a man you would like to have guarding your back.

'So they kicked you out,' Steve said.

Pollinger gave a curt nod. 'I hung around in High Rock for a spell and then I decided to come here. I heard you were sheriff of River Bend and it seemed the best thing to do.'

It didn't seem quite the best thing to do from Steve's point of view. In fact, he figured it might be downright embarrassing for a sheriff harbouring an ex gaol bird. Except that Pete Pollinger had once or twice saved his life, and a man doesn't forget that.

'So you don't have anywhere to stay?'

'Like the foxes and the wolves,' Pollinger croaked. He gave a brief chuckle that turned into a hard cough. 'Sorry about that,' he said.

'Have you seen a sawbones?' Steve asked him.

'I did see one once but he just sold me a bottle of some kind of fizz and told me it would either cure me or kill me.'

As Pollinger coughed into his rag again, Steve looked on amazed. Was this that old buddy of his who had seemed invincible? Now Pete was so emaciated he might soon become invisible!

'We have a very good doctor here,' Steve said. 'I'll fix you up with an appointment. But first, you need a good meal.'

He took Pete Pollinger along to the River Bend Hotel which was open. 'Sit down right here,' he said, indicating his usual table.

As they had walked along Steve had noticed how difficult breathing was for his old amigo. Pete had, in fact, paused to catch his breath several times in spite of the short distance involved.

Now Pollinger sat behind the table, panting slightly and looking relieved.

When Maria appeared she raised her eyebrows slightly. Maria was an astute woman and Steve guessed she recognized Pete Pollinger from the grainy photo in the paper. Then Maria approached their table. 'What can I do for you gentlemen?' she asked.

Steve was still standing. 'This man is a friend of mine. He's just come in on the stage and he needs feeding up.'

Maria looked down at the sick man with some concern. She saw that he looked half-starved. 'I guess you need one of our rare-cooked steaks,' she said.

'Thank you kindly,' the sick man said. 'But I don't eat too much these days on account of I'm sick.'

'I'm sure we can find something that will be wholesome and good,' Maria said. She had poured Pollinger a pint of beer which he gulped down as though he hadn't drank for a year.

When the serving girl brought the meal Pollinger looked down at it and shook his head. 'I'll do my best,' he said before raising his knife and starting to saw at his meat.

While Pollinger was doing his best with the meal, Steve went over to the bar to talk to Maria.

'So you brought him here,' she said.

'Well, Maria, it's like this, he didn't have anywhere else to go. As you might have guessed, the man's sick unto death.'

'What are we going to do with him?' she asked.

Steve shook his head. He had taken on board the word we. 'Well, first I have to get him to Doc MacFadden. After that. . . .'

She gave him a keen look and said, 'After that, what?'

'After that . . . I shall have to think about it.'

Doc MacFadden was fixing a splint on a man's leg when they arrived. Steve and Pete Pollinger sat in the waiting-room and Steve noticed that Pete Pollinger was moving his fingers about restlessly on his knee.

'Don't worry. Doc MacFadden is the best we got here. He doesn't drink except for sarsaparilla. So he has a steady hand.'

Pollinger had no time to respond since, at that moment, a man hobbled out of the surgery with a splint on his leg.

'Afternoon, Sheriff,' the man said to Steve. 'I bust my leg and the doc fixed me up real good.' He continued stump-ing to the door, clucking away to himself.

The next minute Doc MacFadden was standing in the surgery doorway, beckoning to them. 'Come in, gentle-men,' he said.

Pollinger coughed into his hand as they went into the surgery.

Doc MacFadden tapped and listened to Pollinger's heart and his lungs. When it came to the lungs, he listened and shook his head. 'You want the truth?' he asked Pete Pollinger.

'I know the truth,' Pollinger said. 'The truth is I'm dying.'

The doc stepped back and looked at him gravely. 'At

least you're honest with yourself,' he said.

'How long d'you reckon I've got?' Pollinger asked him.

Doc MacFadden shook his head. 'Hard to say. Maybe six months, maybe less.'

'That's what I thought,' Pollinger said fatalistically. 'So there's nothing you can do to help me.'

'I'm afraid you're right, Mr Pollinger. If you rest up and keep your appetite going, you might live longer. If you smoke a lot and drink too much, it'll probably be sooner.'

Pollinger grinned. 'A short life and a gay one,' he said.

'That's about the size of it, Mr Pollinger. The truth is, you've got advanced tuberculosis.'

Pollinger put on his shirt and vest and held his black Stetson in his hand. 'Thanks for the advice, Doc.'

Doc MacFadden looked at Steve and nodded.

Outside the doctor's surgery Pete Pollinger paused to look left and right as though he thought someone might be lurking in a doorway waiting to shadow him.

'Listen. Steve,' he said. 'I should be moving on but the truth is I don't know where to go.'

'Well, the first thing we do is we go back to the office for a bit of jawbone,' Steve said.

Fifteen minutes later they sat across the desk from one another in the sheriff's office.

'You got any whiskey hereabouts?' Pete Pollinger asked.

'Well, I do keep a bottle for medicinal purposes,' Steve admitted, 'but the doc advised you to keep off the booze.'

'That's OK,' Pollinger said. 'You're going to die you might as well die happy.'

Steve reached for the bottle and poured a small measure.

'Why, Steve, you're getting somewhat miserly in your old age. You weren't such a skinflint during the war.'

'Desperate measures,' Steve responded. 'To tell you the truth, I had a bit of a problem after that bloody war. Couldn't sleep nights, so I drank too much. It was Doc MacFadden who persuaded me to give it up. And I feel a whole lot better for it.'

Pollinger threw back his drink and helped himself to another. 'It eases the pain somewhat,' he said. 'When a man is dying he needs some kind of support, you know.'

'Guess so,' Steve responded.

Pollinger studied Steve over his glass. 'See you've still got your hogleg on,' he said.

Steve tapped the butt of his forty-five Colt revolver. 'Don't use it much,' he said. 'But I guess it's part of the job. Convinces people I'm not just a badge.'

'You used to be quite useful with that there cap and ball you used to tote during the war,' Pollinger said. 'You remember that time you saved my life?'

Steve frowned. 'I remember shooting a man who was about to shoot you,' he admitted.

'I can still see him now,' Pollinger reminisced. 'We were in that trench together after the rest of the company had retreated. And that bearded guy suddenly appeared out of nowhere with a shooter – I don't remember what kind it was – and he was about to blow my head off when you turned like lightning and blasted him to hell. You remember that?'

Steve certainly remembered the incident. In fact he was still trying to shake it out of his mind. He saw the man, a captain in the Confederate army, just feet away about to take a shot at Pollinger. He had a big grizzly beard. Steve remembered how the captain's head jerked back when he fired and how he had dropped over the parapet with his face spurting with blood.

That had been a night to celebrate and both Steve and

Pete had got themselves pissed out of their minds.

Steve still remembered the face of that captain blasted to pulp as he jerked back. He and Sergeant Pollinger had both killed many times during that ghastly conflict but none before at such close quarters.

'You know what, Steve,' Pete Pollinger said. 'I wouldn't have been here if you didn't kill that captain. He probably had a wife and children too, but you don't think about that when you're at war, do you.'

That brought on another fit of coughing.

'You need to rest up like the doc says,' Steve advised him when the coughing had subsided.

Pete wiped his mouth clean. 'Things to do,' he said. 'Arrangements to make.' He narrowed his eyes.

'What arrangements had you in mind?' Steve asked.

Pete grinned. 'Arrangements about dollars. Arrangements about you,' he said.

Steve gulped. 'I don't savvy. You're talking in riddles, man.'

'Time to come clean.' Pete sat forward with his elbows on the table. 'Listen, Steve, I have to tell you a few things.'

'Like what things in particular?'

'You know why I was in gaol?' Pete said.

'I don't know much. Just that you did hold-up jobs. Banks mostly.'

'Sure,' Pete nodded. 'And I had a few shootouts. I guess you have too.'

'As sheriff, yes, but only in the line of duty.'

'Well, I had a shootout with the law and they got me in the arm and put me in the slammer to cool me off.'

'I read about that,' Steve said. 'That's what we do with lawbreakers.'

Pete gave him a good natured grin. 'Just like the old

41

times, Steve. You always liked to joke. That's what kept the platoon so happy. They should have made you up to captain, you know that?'

'Thanks for the compliment, but I didn't want captain. I was just glad when the whole shebang was over.' He made a sideways gesture with the flat of his hand. '*Finito!*'

'Well, that's all past history, anyway,' Pete said. 'The fact is, I rode with some pretty ugly characters during that time after the war. You ever heard of Wesley Carradine?'

Steve nodded. 'Seen his face on a wanted poster a while back. I hear he's still at large. There's probably a reward for him, dead or alive.'

'Well, I rode with the Carradine bunch a way back.'

Steve nodded again. Was this confession time? Maybe Pete Pollinger should be talking to Father Sylvester. 'Where are you taking me here?' he asked.

'Where I'm taking you is to the pot of gold at the end of the rainbow. That's where I'm taking you.' He looked at Steve and Steve saw his eyes gleaming with the promise of riches.

'I'm afraid you lost me there, man,' he said.

Pete reached out for the bottle again and took a swig straight from the lip. Steve saw with alarm that the level had now dropped below the halfway line. This man's a rummy, he thought.

'Three things.' Pete held up three fingers. 'Number one, I got dollars stashed away. Number two, I can't use them. Number three, I want you to have those dollars.' He gave Steve an inquiring look.

Steve said nothing.

Pete gave him a toothy grin. 'Oh, I forget, there's a number four.'

'And what is that?' Steve asked.

42

'Number four is Wesley Carradine knows about those dollars and he wants them badly enough to kill.'

What Pete Pollinger had said had thrown Steve into something of a dilemma. Number one, Pete wanted Steve to have the dollars he had accrued. Two, most of those dollars were loot from the various bank robberies Pete had committed. Three, as sheriff, Steve was supposed to uphold the law and not benefit from stolen dollars. And again there was a number four which was that the outlaw Wesley Carradine was keen to get his ugly hands on those dollars which meant there must be a considerable amount of loot involved.

Steve looked at Pete and saw that he was grinning. 'Now, Pete,' he said, 'You've put me in a something of a difficult position here.'

'How come?' Pete said.

'Like this,' Steve said. He held up his right hand and gave Pete the four points, one after the other. After each one, Pete gave a nod.

'I understand what you're saying,' he said, 'and I appreciate it, but think about it like this – if you don't take that money, somebody else will. Once you've got it you can leave it to the dog home or a refuge for calico queens if you prefer.'

Steve chuckled. 'I might like dogs but I don't know about that.' He raised his eyebrows. 'How much are we talking about here, anyway?'

Pete closed one eye and looked up at the ceiling. 'Well, I should guess some fifty.'

'Fifty dollars?' Steve said.

'No,' Pete said, 'Fifty big ones – fifty grand.'

Steve whistled quietly. 'Fifty thousand,' he said.

'Give or take a few,' Pete agreed.

Steve sat back and considered. Fifty thousand dollars

seemed an awfully large sum for a humble sheriff with no future prospects. 'So, where do you keep this loot?' he asked.

'Well, one thing's for sure,' Pete said. 'It ain't under the mattress since I don't have a mattress at the moment.'

You're damned right about that, Steve thought. 'What will you do for tonight,' he said impulsively. 'I have a small room back of the office. You can sleep there tonight.'

'What about you? Where will you sleep?'

'I'll sleep here in one of the cells. As long as I keep the keys with me, nobody can lock me in.' Steve laughed again.

Pete didn't need much convincing since he was dog tired. So a little after sundown he turned in for the night.

Steve sat in the office for a while. He thought about all that loot and where it might be hidden and what a man could do with it in his hands. Then he had a sudden vision of a scarlet-faced demon with horns who must be his majesty the devil himself.

Here comes the tempter, he thought. Steve was no great believer in devils or saints for that matter: some men were relatively good and some were relatively ugly. Everything balanced out in the end. Then he thought of the Jesuit, Father Sylvester. He's the closest I know to being a saint and I guess he'd know what to do, he thought. Then another voice chimed in: the good Father Sylvester would invest all that money in the Jesuit House which might be considered a waste of dollars. But would that be such a bad thing, after all?

Then there came a gentle tap, tap at the door. Steve reached for his shooter and rested it on the table before him. 'Walk right in,' he said.

The door opened quietly and a face peeped in at him.

44

'Why, here you are sitting all alone,' Maria said. 'And with your revolver on the table too.'

'That seemed to be the case,' he agreed. 'Why don't you step right in and join me?'

With a rustle of skirts Maria closed the door and joined him at the table. Though she looked happy enough to see him, Steve sensed she wasn't at ease.

'Is there something on your mind?' he asked her.

'I'm thinking about your amigo,' she said. 'I thought I might find him biding with you here.'

Steve shook his head. 'He's lying in the back room asleep. Dog tired and sick too.'

'You mean you've given up your bed for him?' she asked.

'That's no big deal,' he said. 'He saved my life on more than one occasion during the war. You don't forget about things like that.'

'Then where will you sleep?' she asked.

Steve gestured towards one of the cells. 'In there, I guess.'

Maria looked mildly surprised. 'You can't do that, Steve.'

'Why not? It'll give me a chance to learn how it suits the customers.' He grinned.

Maria looked to one side; she was used to Steve's somewhat wry humour. 'You could come back to the hotel with me,' she offered. 'It'd be a lot more comfortable there.'

When Steve returned her quizzical look, she blushed.

His grin softened to a smile. 'Are you making me an offer I can't refuse?' he asked.

'Not right now,' she laughed. 'I'm just saying you need your sleep.' She paused and looked serious. 'I was talking to the mayor no more than half an hour back and I think he's worried.'

She looked down at the Colt forty-five resting on the

45

table between them.

'About what?' Steve asked.

'About you and that *amigo* of yours.'

'What did the mayor say?'

She shrugged her shoulders. 'He said there are men out there looking for Pete Pollinger and they want to kill him.'

'Not before they get his money,' Steve suggested. Then he caught his breath. Maybe I shouldn't have said that, he thought.

Maria gave him a shrewd look. 'So this friend of yours has money?'

'Pete tells me he's got a heap stashed away. I think he wants me to have it. He has no heirs to consider so he wants to leave it to me before he dies.'

She looked at him wide-eyed. 'But, Steve, you can't take that dirty money. If you play with pitch, it sticks to your hands.'

Steve made no reply. He was thinking about Wesley Carradine and his thugs.

CHAPTER FOUR

Wesley Carradine had a problem, several problems in fact. First, he had a price on his head and he had to keep out of view. Second, he knew Pete Pollinger had been released from gaol but he didn't know where he was. Third, Pete Pollinger had a big sum of money squirrelled away somewhere and Carradine figured that money was rightfully his. And fourth, he would have liked to see Pollinger sprawled in the middle of the broad walk with a hole or two in his head or even swinging from a tree with a rictus of agony on his face.

Right now Carradine was sitting in a small cabin no more than twenty miles from River Bend nursing his grudges. With him were the two half-breed women who attended to all his needs and two of his buddies, Jim Stacy and Greg Nevarro, who were like male versions of the ugly sisters. They didn't look alike but they had worked together so long that they could practically read each other's thoughts. They ate together, and killed together if necessary; so they were more than a mere comedy duo.

Wesley Carradine sat at the table and ate and drank, and nursed his vindictive notions. I'm worth a whole lot more than this, he said to himself. I might not be old but it's time

I retired. And I could have retired if that double-crossing snake Pete Pollinger hadn't stolen the dollars that were rightfully mine.

Though Carradine drank a good deal, he was by no means bloated. He was one of those men who could eat and drink a lot without getting fat. He was still lean and mean-looking and he took a pride in his profile. He shaved even when he didn't need to and watched with pride as those two half-breed women washed and ironed his shirts and prepared his meals. The older of the two females, a woman called Miranda, was a particularly good cook which accounted for the fact that, when she walked, she looked like a galleon in full sail.

The scene in the cabin might have seemed cosy and even Christmassy except that it wasn't Christmas and the place was no more than a neglected cabin and part of an abandoned silver mine project. The three men looked somewhat restless too. Even during mealtimes Stacy and Nevarro cleaned their revolvers relentlessly because they had nothing better to do. Stacy even held his shooter up to the light and spun the chambers.

'Stop waving that thing about, you mutton head,' Carradine said. 'Some day when you do that someone is going to get the wrong impression and shoot you dead.'

'That's the truth,' Nararro said. 'Why can't you keep yourself still and concentrate on your chow?'

Stacy shook his head and holstered his shooter.

Though as vain as Narcissus, Carradine was no fool. He could see that his two sidekicks were longing for action just as he was himself.

'I've been thinking,' he said as they passed the bottle round for the third time.

His two henchmen eyed him suspiciously.

'You've been thinking,' Stacy said accusingly as though thinking might be considered something of a misdemeanour.

'Yes, like thinking,' Nevarro said. 'That's the thing you do with your brain, you know, knucklehead.' He gave a hard barking laugh; Nevarro was proud of his sense of humour.

'What are you thinking?' Stacy asked, looking intently at Wesley Carradine across the table.

'I've been thinking I've got a little mission for you two boys,' Carradine said.

'What mission?' asked Stacy blankly.

'Like a mission is a job you have to do,' Narvarro informed him.

Carradine raised a bony finger and pointed it at Stacy. 'I have a hunch,' he said.

A frown of puzzlement appeared on Stacy's face. 'A hunch,' he said.

Nevarro didn't bother to explain.

'I have a hunch that Pete Pollinger might have headed for the town of River Bend.'

'That's a possibility,' Navarro agreed.

'So, what's with River Bend?' Stacy asked them.

'River Bend is like a place on the river,' Navarro laughed. 'I'm surprised you don't know that, Jimsy boy.'

Stacy glared momentarily at his partner. He hated being called Jimsy boy, thought it made him sound like a pansy. 'OK, what's with River Bend?' he asked. 'I know the place. I've been there before. It's like growing and it'll soon be as big as High Rock. That's what I know about River Bend.'

'What's with River Bend is this,' Carradine said. 'I figure that's where Pollinger might be headed.'

Navarro nodded. 'Sounds reasonable. So what's the deal, Wes?'

'The deal is this, I want you two boys to ride into River Bend and have a look see. Don't attract too much attention to yourselves. Just mosey around and investigate. Stay at one of those cheap hotels for a few days and see what you can find out. Don't get drunk and don't make any kind of ruckus. You're just two wandering hobos looking for a chance to make a living, that's all.'

'That sounds easy enough,' Stacy said. 'Just like a vacation, in fact.'

'This is no vacation,' Navarro explained. 'This is business.'

'That's right,' Carradine agreed. 'What you do is mingle with the crowd and make a few enquiries and, if you find Pete Pollinger, just slip out of town and report back to me. But whatever you do, don't get into any kind of trouble and, number one, don't shoot the guy. I want him alive so he can lead us to that stash of dough. D'you hear what I'm saying to you?'

Stacy's eyes brightened up. 'I get the picture,' he said, 'but what about dollars. I'm clean out right now.' He stood up and pulled out the linings of his pant pockets to prove the point.

'Don't worry about that,' Carradine said. 'I'll shell out enough. You two chuckle-heads just ride into town, keep your noses clean, take a look around and come back in a couple of days. If you catch up with Pete Pollinger, I'll get my head round the question of what to do next.'

Stacy nodded. 'It's a cinch, Wes.'

Carradine gave Navarro the dollars. Though he knew Stacy wasn't as chuckle-headed as he pretended to be he was, to say the least, somewhat flaky.

'And remember,' Carradine said. 'Don't make any trouble. I want Pollinger alive. After we've got our hands on

50

that stash of dollars, he can go to Kingdom Come and back as far as I'm concerned.'

'And we help him on his way too,' Stacy laughed. 'That sounds like a reasonable deal, Wes.'

Some hours later Stacy and Navarro rode into River Bend. The town was growing and all kinds of people were drifting through: gold miners on their way to the hills, sales representatives, cowmen, and men and women in search of every kind of employment. Stacy and Navarro looked like a couple of saddle-bums in search of employment, so they guessed nobody was likely to look at them twice. They wouldn't approach the River Bend Hotel which was far too highfalutin for them. So they rode along Main Street looking for a place to rest up.

'Somewhere a traveller can lay his head?' Stacy asked a man who was sitting in a rocking-chair on the sidewalk.

Solomon Seal, the man, looked up and took out his cob pipe. He looked at the two saddle-bums and summed them up. 'You got dollars to pay?' he asked.

'We got enough,' Navarro said.

Solomon Seal looked them up and down and noticed that, though they seemed to be saddle-bums, they were well tooled up with artillery. He gestured to the right with his pipe. 'Try Little Nell's place just off the main drag a few yards up from here. They've usually got space. They take in all manner of people.' He said the 'all manner of people' with a gleam of contempt in his eyes.

Stacy and Navarro rode on without a thank you. 'They ain't none too friendly in this town,' Stacy said to Navarro.

'We don't do friendly,' Navarro replied. 'We're here to find a man, so don't get your dander up.'

Stacy clamped his jaw tight. Though he thought

51

Navarro's reasoning was somewhat faulty he decided to say nothing.

Just off the main drag they found Little Nell's place. They dismounted, tied their horses to the hitching-rail and walked inside. The interior was full of acrid smoke and there was a crowd of men and women standing around, puffing away in a haze of cheap tobacco smoke. Behind the counter was a man wearing a well-stained apron.

'Are you Little Nell?' Stacy asked him.

The man with the stained apron looked down at him and sneered. 'Do I look like a woman?' he said.

That caused a guffaw of laughter from the people standing at the bar.

Stacy drew aside his coat to expose his gun holster, but Navarro elbowed him to one side and stepped up to the bar. 'What my friend means is do you have a room where we can stay?'

'How long?' the man behind the bar enquired laconically.

'It don't matter how long,' Stacy said, 'and it don't matter how wide either. It's just have you got a room?'

The man behind the bar looked down at him again. 'How long will you be requiring the room?'

'No more than two days, possibly three,' Navarro said. Then the man quoted a figure.

Stacy frowned and Navarro nodded. 'That'll be OK,' he said.

'In advance,' the man added.

Before Stacy could say anything more, Navarro shelled out the necessary coins.

The room they were shown into was by no means wholesome. It had a mixture of strange smells like stale tobacco smoke, rotting food, and various other unmentionable odours.

'What a dump!' Stacy said.

Navarro had to agree: the place did stink. 'Remember what Wes said. Try to look like a run-down cowpoke which is what you are, and don't start kicking up a ruckus. We just have to locate this *hombre* Pollinger, if he's in town.'

'You mean we just sit here drinking cheap booze and eating rotten food for two days?' Stacy complained.

'I didn't mean literally. I mean like we keep our heads low and ask around about this Pollinger guy.'

Stacy wasn't satisfied. 'Well, I don't altogether agree with that,' he said. 'I figure we don't come into town much and we might as well make the best of it. We could visit with one or two girls of the line and maybe drop in on a game of poker or two.'

'You start drinking and playing poker you might as well be burning your money and we don't have that much, do we?' Navarro retorted.

Stacy gave a low chuckle. 'We might have a little more than you think. I have a little poke of my own tucked away. I lay it out on the cards I might increase it by one hundred per cent or more.'

'More like you throw it on the trash heap,' Navarro replied.

Stacy didn't agree with that; he was in an optimistic mood despite the stinking room and the smoky bar. 'And another thing,' he said. 'If we mingle around and use our ears we might find out something about this Pollinger character.'

Navarro shrugged his shoulders. He was already beginning to think he should have ridden into River Bend on his own.

*

They left their room, pushed their way through the bar and went outside to retrieve their horses and take them to the livery stable. They mounted up and rode back to the main drag where Solomon Seal, the man with the cob pipe, sat smoking on the sidewalk.

As they were about to pass him, he raised his pipe and grinned. 'Satisfied?' he sang out.

'About what?' Stacy said.

'About Little Nell's place. Did they fix you up good?'

'They fixed us up reasonable,' Stacy replied. 'The place is a dump.'

Solomon Seal laughed contemptuously. 'What did you expect, The Grand Metropolitan Hotel?'

The two travellers had stopped. Navarro tipped his Stetson. 'You happen to have heard of a man called Pollinger?' he asked politely.

'Pollinger, did you say?'

'Pete Pollinger.'

'What sort of business is he in?'

'We thought he might have drifted into town recently,' Navarro said.

Solomon Seal laughed. 'This town is growing, mister. People come drifting in and drifting out all the time, just like rain clouds. What d'you want this Pollinger for, anyway?' He looked at the two riders and took note of their holstered weapons again.

'A matter of business,' Navarro informed him.

'Try the Fargo office,' Solomon Seal said.

Navarro tipped his Stetson again. 'Thank you kindly, sir.'

'And by the way,' Stacy chipped in. 'Is there a livery stable close by?'

Solomon Seal pointed along the street with his cob pipe. 'Just a piece down there.'

Solomon Seal watched the two men riding down Main Street to the livery stable. One was tall and lean and the other was plump and more comfortable-looking. Yet the more comfortable *hombre* was the meaner of the two and the leaner one was more polite. They were both wearing shooters in well-worn holsters and he figured they were up to no good.

Solomon Seal had lived in River Bend a good long time and had seen the town grow. Some of the things he saw, he approved of; others were not so good. He knocked out his pipe and walked up the street until he came to the River Bend Hotel. He walked into the restaurant and bar room and saw Sheriff Steve Carrington and Maria sitting at Steve's usual table drinking beer together. He ordered a beer at the bar and took it over to the table. Things were building up and Maria was about to go and attend to her customers.

'Good day, Maria,' Solomon Seal said, tipping his hat.

'Good day to you, Solomon,' she said with half a curtsey.

As she moved away Solomon looked down at the sheriff.

'See you got yourself a beer, Solomon,' the sheriff said. 'Why don't you sit yourself down and join me before I go back to my office.'

'Much obliged, Steve.' Solomon pulled out a chair and sat down.

'Something on your mind, Sol?' Steve asked him. They had known one another from even before Steve had taken up the sheriff's badge and Steve knew how Solomon had sat in his chair with nothing much to do except to watch the world go by. Solomon, like his namesake, observed almost everything that happened in the town. He owned Little Nell's place. In fact Nell was the name of his wife. The small hotel that Stacy had called 'a dump' made a reasonable profit, so he didn't complain.

'Well, not much,' Solomon replied to the question, 'except that two hombres have just hit town. They look like saddle-tramps but they're carrying guns and they asked me if I knew a man called Pete Pollinger.'

Steve was sitting back in his chair and showed no particular surprise at this information, though anyone studying him closely might have noticed a slight flickering of his eyebrows. 'And what did you say to them?' he asked.

'I told them I had never heard of the guy.' Of course, that wasn't strictly true. Solomon Seal spent quite a lot of time studying the newspapers and he had read about Pete Pollinger's recent release from gaol.

Steve raised his mug and sipped his coffee slowly. Then he placed his mug on a mat on the table and nodded. 'Thanks for the information, Sol. I appreciate it.'

After they had found the livery stable and fixed up a price, Stacy and Navarro stepped out on to Main Street again. Stacy looked across the street and saw a sign that read 'The Big Gaming House'. Underneath there was a small inscription with the legend 'Come inside and win with us'.

Navarro gave a curt laugh. 'That's a damned hoot. The house wins and everyone else loses.'

Stacy was studying the sign intently. 'You're a true pessimist, Nav. The lucky man wins.'

Navarro grinned but he wasn't happy. He knew about Stacy and his wild nature. 'Why don't we take a bath and go in search of those ladies of the line?' he suggested.

Stacy was still looking at the sign. 'You go have your bath. Lie there deep and snooze a while. I'll join you later back at Little Nell's. I'm just going to mosey over and take a look in that gaming house, see what I can see.'

Navarro shrugged. 'Well, as long as you remember what we're here for. Nothing more and nothing less than investigating about that Pollinger guy. And don't cause a ruckus with anyone.'

Stacy gave a curt nod and headed over the street to the promise of The Big Gaming House where you could win or lose a fortune.

Navarro decided not to head back to Little Nell's place since he figured that if a man took a bath there he'd come out dirtier than he went in. The moonlight was shining optimistically. So he started sauntering down Main Street inspecting the premises. Since he was here some years back the place had grown considerably. Some of the stores were quite fancy but one in particular attracted his attention. It was called The Sunshine Parlour. Outside were several ladies with parasols sporting themselves under the ramada. Since there was no sunshine the parasols were nothing but cosmetic but they worked their spell well enough in the mysterious light from the oil lamps. One of the ladies peeped at him from under her shade and smiled invitingly.

'You new in town?' she asked with an enticing lisp.

Navarro tipped his Stetson and the ladies laughed. 'Do you know of a place where a man can take a bath?' he asked.

The lady who had spoken tilted her parasol again. 'We can arrange for that, mister. We have a very clean house here. Why don't you just step inside?' She rose from her chair and motioned towards the entrance.

Navarro hesitated for no more than a moment. Then he stepped inside and looked around. To a man who spent so much time in rough country with rough people it seemed like paradise.

The girl who was, on closer inspection, a good deal more than a girl, wafted a strange perfume over him. 'My name's Juliet,' she said with her not unattractive lisp. 'Walk right through here and I'll fix that bath for you. As I said we run a clean house here. We all take a bath at least once a week and sometimes more often.'

Navarro liked the lilt of her voice; he thought she came from somewhere east, possibly France or even England or Italy.

'What is your name, sir?' she asked liltingly.

'Just call me Nav,' he said.

'Nav. That's a very fine name, kind of friendly,' she lilted. 'Why don't you just sit down and relax a while and I'll tell you when your bath is ready. Do you read magazines, sir?'

Navarro had no idea what a magazine was but he could read without moving his lips so he figured he was an educated man. 'I think I'll just sit here and think,' he said.

'Yes, indeed,' Juliet said. 'I like a thinking man and I'll tell you when your bath is ready, sir.'

Jim Stacy stood in the doorway of The Big Gaming House and looked around. The place wasn't quite as large as he had expected, but it looked inviting to a man who had a taste for gambling. There were a number of tables deployed around the room, most of them occupied by men playing five-card stud and five-card draw. Between the tables were lightly clad and heavily made-up women, serving drinks and chatting to the punters whenever they could.

A man in a dark jacket and trousers and a fancy vest welcomed Stacy with a smile. 'Good evening, sir. Are you looking to take a hand in a game of poker, sir?'

'Could be,' Stacy replied.

The man looked him over appraisingly yet, despite

Stacy's hobo-like appearance, did not appear to be unduly concerned. 'There is just one thing, sir,' he said in a somewhat wheedling tone.

'What's that?' Stacy asked him bluntly.

The man smiled. 'Well, it's like this, sir, we don't encourage the wearing of firearms in this establishment.'

'Is that so?' Stacy said.

The man blinked and Stacy saw that he had a black moustache with waxed ends. What a pansy, he thought.

Navarro lay back in his bath and wallowed. This is one hell of a good life, he reflected as Juliet and one of the other ladies poured warm water over him and Juliet scrubbed his back. The bath water was deep and he could have lain there all night luxuriating and reflecting if there hadn't been other matters to consider.

A voice aroused him suddenly. 'I've brought you a drink,' Juliet said, holding out a tray. 'I'll put it here right beside you, compliment of the house.'

Compliment of my arse, Navarro said to himself. But what the hell, I'm in fairyland. He reached out lazily and took the glass and drained its contents. Brandy, he thought, the best brandy I ever tasted. And within minutes he was asleep.

Stacy stared at the man with the black moustache with waxed ends and grinned as he patted his gun-holster with his hand. 'I'd like to take a hand of cards but it's like this, mister, this Colt pistol and me are never apart. He's like my best friend. I even sleep with it.'

A nervous grin flitted across the man's face. 'In that case, sir,' he said, 'I don't think we can help you. Rule of the house, you see.' He looked into Stacy's eyes and started to blink; it was clear he saw something he didn't like in the depth of Stacy's eyes.

Next second a big beefy fellow came and stood by the man's side. He had his shirt sleeves rolled up and Stacy saw huge bulging biceps with naked women tattooed on them. 'We don't take guns in here,' he said in a deep mocking tone.

Navarro shook his head and roused himself. In the nick of time: next second he would have dunked himself into the deep water and possibly choked to death. He had read of a man who had been partly drugged and then had his head pushed under. So he woke in something of a panic.

After he had spluttered and spewed out the water in his mouth, he opened his eyes and saw the perfumed woman Juliet smiling down at him like an angel of mercy.

'I think you might have dropped off for a minute or two,' she said with a smile.

The water was cooling rapidly; so he knew that his nap had taken more than a minute or two. Juliet was holding out a voluminous towel with red and white stripes. 'You want to get out now?' she invited.

'Seems like a good idea,' he said. Am I in heaven? he asked himself, as he shook himself down and stepped out onto the bath mat.

Juliet and her assistant threw the towel over him and started rubbing him down.

'I think you've done this before,' he laughed.

'Only to our most favoured customers,' she said, rubbing harder and more deftly. 'Now I think you might lie down for a while and take a rest,' she said.

Navarro didn't think he needed a rest; rather the opposite. In fact: the ladies with the bath towel seemed to have stimulated every nerve in his body.

They led him out of the bathhouse and into a room where the rich perfume that he had smelled around Juliet's body was even stronger and more overpowering. Am I being drugged? he asked himself, but it didn't seem to matter, anyway. He lay down on the bed and suddenly realized that Juliet was undressing and ready to lie down beside him.

'I think I'm at heaven's gate,' he said aloud.

'Let's make it good,' she said quietly.

'I've got good money here,' Stacy said. He had a high temper and the big man with the tattooed biceps brought the blood to his head.

'Rule of the house,' the big man announced in his base voice.

Stacy looked past him and saw the faces of the card players staring in their direction with surprise and anticipation; the man with the waxed moustache had his mouth half open as though he thought he was about to experience something that would both shock and excite him.

The sight of that waxed moustache and that shocked expression fired Stacy up and he made a move forward as if to push past the big man into the gaming area.

Before he could step right into the hall, the big man's hand shot out to restrain him. 'Like I said, we've got rules here,' he said.

'To hell with your rules!' Stacy hissed, pressing harder against the outsized hand.

The big man brought his left fist across and clipped Stacy on the side of the jaw. Though it wasn't more than a tap to the big man, Stacy's head jerked sideways, sending him reeling against the door jam.

Flames of fury leaped up in Stacy's head. He made a move to recover himself but, before he could lash out at the big man, the big man seized him by the shoulders and spun him round. Then he gave Stacy a huge push that propelled him across the sidewalk and on to Main Street where he plunged forward into the dust.

He lay there for a moment, shaking his head and spitting out the dust and then spun round and reached for his gun. He was quick on the draw but not quite quick enough.

'Hell's bells!' the big man shouted, dodging behind the door.

'My God!' the man with the waxed moustache cried as he flung himself to one side.

Stacy fired a single shot but the bullet went wide and lodged itself in the woodwork above the door, close to the sign that said The Big Gaming House.

Stacy scrambled to his feet, ready to fire a second shot but, before he could yank back the hammer, a voice came from his right. 'Drop that gun!' it said.

Stacy turned to see a tall man with a gun pointing at him. The tall man moved forward and kicked out at him.

Stacy took the kick right on the shoulder. He might have fired another shot but again it was too late. The next second, the man's revolver was pressed against his temple. 'Drop it!' the man said.

Stacy let his gun fall from his hand. 'OK, sheriff, you win!' he said.

Steve Carrington kicked the gun away and hauled the man to his feet. 'Disturbing the peace,' he said. 'Nobody likes the peace to be disturbed in River Bend.'

CHAPTER FIVE

Steve Carrington still had his gun on Jim Stacy. 'Now walk right on,' he said as though he was talking to his horse. 'Keep your hands away from your body and don't bother to pull up your boots either.' Steve knew the tricks of the trade; often these shady characters kept a derringer or a knife inside their boots in case of emergency.

Stacy walked on with his hands raised ahead of him. 'Where are we going?' he asked. He was still breathing hard.

A number of people had stopped to rubber-neck. Everybody likes a good drama. The big man stood grinning with his arms folded and the man with the waxed moustache was tittering nervously.

'I'm taking you to the cells so you calm down a little,' Steve informed the gunman.

'But I've booked a room in Little Nell's place,' Stacy protested.

'Well, you can kiss goodbye to that,' Steve said as he stooped to retrieve Stacy's gun. He stuck the gun through his own gunbelt and prodded Stacy in the back.

The sheriff's office was no more than a hundred and fifty yards down Main Street. When they arrived at the office

Steve ordered Stacy to turn round and empty his pockets on to the desk. 'You can't do that,' Stacy protested. 'It's daylight robbery.'

'Apart from the fact that it's dark,' Steve said, 'you put your valuables on the desk and I'll give you a receipt for them. When I unlock the cell come sun-up I'll dish them back to you before I run you out of town.'

Stacy went on complaining as he emptied his pockets and laid the contents on the desk: a gold watch and chain, a surprising number of dollar pieces, a small knife, and not much more. 'Now write that all down if you can write and I'll sign the paper. Is that good enough for you?' Steve asked him.

'What, you think I can't read and write?' Stacy said hotly.

'I have no idea about your educational accomplishments, so I wouldn't like to speculate on that.' Steve handed him a pen and Stacy wrote the list in a surprisingly copperplate hand. 'I see you're a man of education,' Steve told him as he signed the list and put the gunman's possessions into a bag and the bag into a drawer.

'What about my shooter?' Stacy asked. 'That wasn't on the list.'

Steve grinned. 'You'll have to trust me on that one.' He paused. 'By the way, I think I forgot to ask you your name.'

Stacy shook his head. 'You can call me Hank Hardwick.'

Steve was still grinning somewhat skeptically. 'Well now, Mr Hank Hardwick, why don't you just step into that comfortable cell there and retire for the night? Come sun-up we will review your case.'

Stacy looked hard into the sheriff's opaque eyes for a moment and then shrugged. He turned towards the cells and noticed that the one on the right had been recently occupied.

'Take the one on the left,' Steve said. 'Tuck right down and think about the tooth fairy.'

Stacy stepped into the cell and took a look; he wasn't too pleased with what he saw, but there wasn't much use arguing. So, as Steve locked the door, he sat down on the bed, pulled off his boots and shook the dust on to the floor of the cell, and stretched out on the wheezy cot.

Steve emptied out the shells of Stacy's Colt revolver and pushed it into a drawer. He turned towards the door that led through to his own quarters and saw a face peering at him through the crack. The door was a little to the right of the cells and recessed back, so a man in the cells couldn't see through to the sheriff's quarters.

The door opened a little further and Pete Pollinger reached out and beckoned to Steve. Steve nodded and went through, closing the door behind him.

Pete Pollinger put a skinny finger to his lips and whispered: 'You know who that hombre is?'

'Says he's Hank Hardwick,' Steve said.

'Hank Hardwick my arse!' Pete Pollinger hissed. 'That's Jim Stacy, one of Carradine's sidekicks.'

Steve showed no surprise. 'I had a hunch he might be,' he said.

They went through to Steve's quarters and Steve told Pollinger about the incident outside The Big Gaming House.

'Where's Navarro?' Pete Pollinger asked Steve.

Steve rubbed his stubbly chin. 'I don't know any Navarro,' he said. Then he remembered what Solomon Seal had said: there were two of them staying at Little Nell's place.

'You savvy what this means, don't you, Steve?' Pollinger said.

'I savvy real well,' Steve replied. 'It means these two scallywags have come into town to nose you out on behalf of the big cheese Wesley Carradine.'

Pete Pollinger made as if to say more, but at that moment, they heard the sound of someone talking in the office.

Navarro had been sound asleep in bed for more than an hour. It was as though the woman Juliet had put some kind of enchantment on him to keep him subdued. When he suddenly woke up he found he was alone and his clothes had vanished.

'What the hell?' he said to himself. He groped towards the door and threw it open. There was no sign of the woman Juliet but there was a man out there, apparently waiting for him.

'You looking for something?' the man asked. Navarro saw that he wasn't tall, no more than five eight, but he was squat and brawny.

'I'm looking for my clothes,' Navarro said.

The man pointed to a stuffed-over chair. 'Would these be them?'

Navarro snatched up his jacket and felt in the pockets but there was no sign of his wallet. He reached for his pants with the same result. 'Where's my money?' he asked.

'What money?'

'The money I had in my wallet.'

The squat man shrugged. 'I think you'll find your wallet out on the desk, waiting for you.'

Navarro went through to the desk followed closely by the man. One of the heavily made-up women handed him his wallet. Navarro flipped it open and there was only a couple of dollars. 'Where's my dollars?' he asked.

'What dollars?'

'The dollars I had when I came in here.'

The squat man gave a kind of smirk. 'I'm afraid that's all that's left, my man. You have to pay for your pleasures, sir. Didn't you learn that yet?'

'Where's Juliet?' Navarro asked him.

The squat man's smirk turned to a grin of contempt. 'I'm afraid Juliet isn't available. She's gone to meet with her Romeo.'

Navarro was fastening the buckle of his gunbelt and the man watched him cautiously. I could shoot this hombre down right where he stands, Navarro thought. The man was watching him closely and reading his thoughts.

'I shouldn't try anything foolish,' he said. 'We don't like foolishness in this town.' There was a glint of menace in his eyes and there were many dark corners in the room from where somebody might easily be drawing a bead on Navarro.

'Shall I tell you something?' Navarro said.

The man laughed. 'Sure, I've always been keen on fairy tales.'

Navarro finished buckling on his gunbelt. His hand was close to his revolver and he could have drawn it and held the man up and demanded his money. But then he thought of Carradine's warning: don't cause a ruckus; just find out if Pete Pollinger is in town.

He turned to the squat man with the long arms and said, 'You better look at me and remember because I will be back to make you fry.'

He turned and went through to the entrance and stepped on to Main Street. He was fuming and he was tempted to turn and shoot a few rounds at the pretty lights along the front of the bordello.

*

He took a few steps down Main Street and suddenly wondered where Jim Stacy could be. It was nearly midnight but people were still milling around in town. He could see the lemon-tinted lights in the windows of The River Bend Hotel and, further along, the lights of the The Big Gaming House.

Time to go back to Little Nell's place, he thought. Stacy is more than probably tucked up in that flea-bitten bed by now.

The bar in Little Nell's was still crowded with men and women, smoking foul smelling cigarettes and throwing back whiskey from the bottle. Navarro elbowed his way to the bar where the barman was pushing bottles of hooch along it.

'Did you see my partner?' Navarro asked.

'I didn't see him but I heard about him,' the man said. 'You want to see him you'll have to look in the hoosegow.'

'The hoosegow?' What had Stacey been doing? You can't trust that guy anywhere, he thought.

The barman leaned forward and shouted out the news about Stacy, how he had tried to shoot up The Big Gaming House an hour or two back and how the sheriff had arrested him and marched him at gunpoint him down to the gaol.

'He's more than probably rattling the bars right now,' a man laughed.

'Like a monkey in a cage,' another man added with a cackle.

'That damned hell raiser!" Navarro muttered. 'What hell's name do I do now?'

Steve Carrington went through to the office and saw Mayor Shapley there, talking to Jim Stacy who was pressed against the bars of his cell.

'It's all one big mistake,' Stacy was trying to explain to the mayor.

'I'm surprised to see you, Mr Mayor,' Steve Carrington said. 'Especially at this time of night.'

'Couldn't sleep,' Mayor Shapley explained. 'Mrs Shapley kicked me right out of the house because I was mooching about so much. So I thought I might come over and see how you're faring.' He sat down at Steve's desk with his back to the door to the street. He got out his tobacco pouch and rolled himself a cigarette. 'Town's getting a damned sight too big to control. Good for business but not so good for crime. You need a deputy, Steve.'

'Well, that's probably true,' Steve conceded. He too was concerned about crime in the town and places like The Big Gaming House and that place opposite where the calico queens and their handlers cheated men out of their dollars. How could you expect a town to be peaceful in those circumstances?

'And another thing,' the mayor said. 'I don't like you to be sleeping in the cell out here. That means you have only one cell free for the law breakers. A sheriff shouldn't be deprived of his bed for an amigo even if he is sick.'

Steve put his finger to his lips and the mayor shook his head.

Jim Stacy was still at the bars of his cell and he was listening intently. The mayor had quite a loud carrying voice and Stacy had sharp ears. Though he had a fiery temper and was quick on the draw he wasn't stupid and he could put two and two together and make less than five. He had heard the sheriff talking to somebody in the back and he wondered who it could be. Could that be Pete Pollinger? he wondered.

*

Navarro lay down on his bed and tried to think. Should he go right down to the sheriff's office and force the sheriff at gunpoint to release the prisoner or hang around till sun-up, hoping things might change? After all, what were they there for if it wasn't to find out whether Pete Pollinger was in town? If they went back to Carradine without learning the truth he was going to make things very hard for them. And, anyway, they wanted to know the truth as much as Carradine because, according to Carradine, there was big money involved.

As he lay on the flea-bitten mattress trying to figure things out he dropped right off to sleep. He had a series of muddled dreams and woke with a start just as the moon was dropping below the horizon and daylight was beginning to creep through the threadbare curtains into his room. He got up, pulled on his pants and checked his Colt revolver. As he did so he remembered the way he had been cheated in the bordello just round the corner. Had he been Stacy he might have checked out his horse at the livery stable and shot up the bordello and all those fancy ladies sitting outside on the porch and especially the squat fellow with the long arms. It would have been highly satisfying to see him dancing around amidst a hail of bullets.

But that wasn't Navarro's style. Be polite, he said to himself; revenge can wait. After we got our hands on Pete Pollinger's stash of dollars we can cut back and shoot the place up.

He grinned to himself and walked downstairs to the bar which still stank abominably.

The bartender was sitting behind the bar with a newspaper propped up in front of him. When Navarro appeared he looked round the paper with a sardonic grin. 'Did you sleep well, mister?' he asked sarcastically.

Navarro shrugged. 'Apart from the fleas I slept pretty good. By the way, did anyone tell you it stinks like armpits and arses in here?'

The barman gave a short bark of laughter. 'You could be a poet,' he said in quite an amiable tone. He took such language as a compliment. 'By the way, when you were out whoring last night, I heard something that might be of interest to you.'

Navarro pricked up his hairy ears. 'And what was that?' he asked.

'Heard you were asking around about that tearaway, Pete Pollinger,' the barman said. 'I been reading about him in this old rag here.'

This is where politeness slots in, Navarro thought. 'A friend of mine would like to know where Pollinger is,' he said, as though it didn't matter too much either way.

'Well, I happened to hear he came in by Wells Fargo the other day.'

Navarro took good note of that. 'You know where he is right now?'

'As to that I don't rightly know. Except that the sheriff, Steve Carrington, met him at the Wells Fargo station and he and Pollinger took a meal together over at The River Bend Hotel.' The barman wrinkled his nose as he mentioned The River Bend Hotel. 'That's that high-falutin place just over the street.'

'I think I'll just take a bite of breakfast,' Navarro said.

'Have it on Little Nell,' the barman said, conveniently forgetting that Navarro had paid in cash for the whole deal the night before. 'Egg and ham do you?' he added.

'That'll be twice,' Navarro said, 'since my partner

checked in with me.'

The barman chuckled again. He had his own reasons for disliking Steve Carrington. He had been one of the men who had supported the boy's hanging after the attempted hold-up at The River Bend Hotel. In fact he was one of Brig Bailey's buddies and he had seen Brig butted in the chest and knocked down on Main Street by Steve Carrington. He didn't care too much for Mayor Shapley either. Some years earlier he had stood for sheriff himself. So he was always glad to stir things up with any long spoon he could lay his hands on.

Navarro had to admit that his big breakfast of ham and eggs was excellent. He even shook hands with the Little Nell's barman and said he had enjoyed it. After breakfast he took a quick drink of whiskey and walked out on to the sidewalk, just in time to see his partner Jim Stacy ambling down Main Street in front of Steve Carrington who was on horseback. They were headed for the livery stable.

Navarro pulled his hat down over his eyes and drew back into the doorway just as Stacy glanced in his direction. Then they were gone.

Navarro eased his Colt revolver in its holster to check that it was free. He walked to the end of the side street and glanced to the right in time to see the sheriff and Stacy disappeared into the livery stable. He stopped to light a quirly and then squatted down on a convenient bench on the sidewalk.

After a few minutes, Stacy and the sheriff emerged from the livery stable and now Stacy was mounted on his horse.

Navarro watched from under the ramada as the two rode by, Stacy slightly ahead of the sheriff. Navarro noticed that Stacy didn't have his gunbelt on.

'What do you aim to do?' Stacy asked the sheriff over his shoulder.

'That's for me to know and for you to find out,' Stave Carrington answered cryptically. 'Just keep riding on like I said.'

Stacy jogged on, past the sheriff's office and past the various stores to the end of town.

'Where to now?' Stacy threw over his shoulder again when they reached the dusty track that led on towards High Rock.

'Now you just keep riding on to wherever you're going,' Steve said. 'It makes no nevermind to me as long as you don't show up in River Bend again. I should warn you, if I ever see you in town again, you'll be back in gaol; that's for your own good and for the good of everyone in town. Do you savvy that?' Steve sounded calm but firm.

Jim Stacy swung round this horse face the sheriff. 'What about my belongings?' he said.

'You got your belongings,' Steve answered tersely.

'What about my shooter. You still got my shooter and my gunbelt.'

'Well, my!' Steve said. 'I forgot about those.' He took the gunbelt and the revolver from in front of him and threw them on the ground.

Stacy looked down where they lay with an expression of disgust and dismay. Then he dismounted and took up his gunbelt. He checked his gun and the gunbelt. 'Where are the shells?' he asked. 'You took the shells from my gun and the belt. Don't they count?'

'They count for a lot,' Steve replied. 'You think I'm naive or something? Now just get on your horse and keep riding and don't come back here again.'

Stacy looked about at the wilderness and before him and threw up his hands in dismay. Then he mounted up and swung his horse round towards Steve. 'Let me tell you something,' he said. 'If you think this is the end of the matter, think again.'

'Can I take that as a threat?' Steve asked him.

'Take it any way you like,' Stacy replied.

That was when they heard the shot.

After Navarro saw Stacy and the sheriff ride out of town, he walked down to the livery stable to collect his horse.

The old geek who looked after the horses led Navarro through to the stables where the horse was munching on hay.

'This horse of yourn has a mighty fine appetite,' the old geek said. 'He's been eating me out of house and home. I'm glad you're here to take him.'

Navarro led his horse out of its stall and paid the man what he could. Owing to the robbery at the bordello, that wasn't much.

The old geek looked at the money and said, 'That's not enough, mister. You owe me more.'

Navarro patted the side of his gun holster, 'That's all you're getting right now. You'll have to wait till I'm next in town on account of I was stripped clean by those calico queens and their *amigos.*'

'In which case I've been cheated,' the old geek replied.

'That's not cheating, that's deferred payment.' Navarro's hand was now resting on the butt of his shooter.

'Like you said,' the old man said. 'Deferred payment.' He spat into the straw fatalistically and turned away.

Navarro was in an ugly mood as he looked towards the

sheriff's office and saw the sheriff and Stacy disappearing into the distance. Once more he was tempted to turn around and shoot up the bordello but again, he thought, that can wait; I've got other things on my mind.

Looking to his left he saw Solomon Seal grinning at him from under the ramada. 'Good morning to you,' Seal sang out, He was manoeuvring his rocking-chair into position but it was a little too early and too cool to sit out there warming his face.

Navarro drew rein but made no reply.

'I see you noticed your buddy riding along there with the sheriff. That was a mighty fool thing he did last night tangling with those people over at The Big Gaming House. Lucky he didn't get himself killed. Now Sheriff Carrington is doing the right thing, running him out of town. You got any sense you'll ride out after him.'

Navarro tipped his Stetson and said nothing. He just urged his horse forward down Main Street and cut off down a side street so he could ride out of town by a less obtrusive route.

Pete Pollinger was eating a sparse breakfast in an upstairs room at the River Bend Hotel when he looked out and saw Navarro and Solomon Seal speaking together across the street. He gave a start and stood up closer to the window. 'Well, I'll be damned,' he said quietly.

Maria was in the room with him. 'What is it?' she asked in surprise. They had come to an arrangement. Pete would slip out by the back door of the sheriff's office, ride down a back street, and enter the hotel by a back door so as not to attract unwanted attention.

'Well, that's Greg Navarro, unless I'm mistaken,' Pollinger said. 'He's Jim Stacy's partner and he's looking towards the end of town where Steve is riding Stacy out of town. That makes my thumb twitch, 'cause I figure he's up to no good.' He sprang up from the table and buckled on his gunbelt.

'Where are you going?' Maria said. 'You haven't finished your breakfast yet.'

Pollinger waved his hand impatiently and started to cough. 'Thanks, Maria, but there's no time for breakfast. I got work to do and it can't wait.'

Maria looked on in dismay as he took up his hat, grabbed his Winchester, and made for the stairs.

Pete Pollinger was coughing again and spitting into a rag as he reached the bottom of the stairs and flung open the door. He paused for a second to catch his breath and then sprang on his horse. Partners in arms, he said to himself as he cut along the backs of cabins and on into the scrub, fighting for the higher ground.

Stop coughing! he said to himself. Concentrate on what needs to be done. Watch out for that slippery customer Greg Navarro.

When he reached the higher ground, he looked down and saw two figures right on the edge of town on the road to High Rock. One was Steve Carrington and the other was Jim Stacy. But there was no sign of that slippery customer Greg Navarro.

Navarro was, in fact, quite close to Pete Pollinger. He had reached the end of town behind the cabins. He dismounted and tethered his horse to a decaying fence-post. He then drew his Winchester and sidled to the end of the cabin and peered out. And he was surprised. He saw Steve Carrington and Jim Stacy talking together. Steve was mounted and Stacy was crouching slightly to the right of him, buckling on his gunbelt. Navarro knew at the range he might miss the

76

sheriff and accidentally cut down his partner.

'Dammit!' he said to himself. 'I've got to get in closer.' So he crouched down and ran forward from sagebrush to sagebrush until he reached a favourable spot. Now Stacy had mounted up and turned away from the sheriff. 'That's perfect.' Navarro muttered to himself. He levered his Winchester, steadied the stock against his shoulder, held his breath, and fired.

It was at that moment that Pete Pollinger caught sight of Navarro crouching behind the sagebrush. He heard the shot and saw Steve Carrington rear up in his saddle and fall. The sight of his army buddy jerking and falling like that brought a rage of blood to Pete Pollinger's head and he fired directly at Navarro. Navarro fell headlong and wriggled like a lizard for cover. Then he crouched down behind another bush and saw Pete Pollinger making ready to fire another shot.

I'll kill the bastard! Navarro said to himself. He levered his Winchester and fired two more shots at Pete Pollinger but Pollinger didn't hang about waiting to be killed. He spurred his mount out of the thicket and bore down on Navarro, firing as he went.

Navarro levered his Winchester and fired twice more. He was about to lever his Winchester for a third time when one of Pollinger's shots hit him right in the head, and he fell back, his head spurting blood among the bushes.

Pete Pollinger wasted no time checking that Navarro was dead. He just rode on to where Steve Carrington was lying close to his horse. As he dismounted he noted that Jim Stacy was no more than a receding dark blob in a cloud of dust.

CHAPTER SIX

Wesley Carradine was standing just outside the cabin on the hill close to the played-out silver mine. He was looking down towards the trail that led from River Bend to High Rock. From where he stood the trail was invisible though he could occasionally see the dust rising when the Wells Fargo stage threaded its way down into the arroyo. Good place for a hold-up, he often said to himself.

The stouter of his two female companions was sweeping dust away from the porch. Sweep ... sweep ... sweep, Carradine thought. When will that damned woman get tired of sweeping? This is too much of a dump to waste your time on sweeping. But why should he complain? The young more attractive woman was inside working on a chicken casserole. Carradine was in clover; he was like a cock with two hens. Yet at this moment he was far from contented. As he stared out in the direction of the trail he was thinking of all the money that sidewinder Pete Pollinger had cheated him out of. 'If I knew where that slippery skookum was at, I could hang him up by his heels, grab him by the throat, and force the truth out of him,' he declared.

The picture of Pete Pollinger dangling by his heels choking out the dust in his lungs gave Carradine a tingle of pleasure and he emitted a low rumble of malicious laughter.

The stout woman looked up and stared at him as though he were mad. 'You crazy, Wes?' she said in a deep masculine-sounding tone.

'Crazy, my arse!' he said, kicking out at a passing tumbleweed.

'You don't want to let yourself get fretted up about these things,' she said. 'It ain't no good for the blood system.'

'What the hell do you know about the blood system?' he retorted. 'You're just an ignorant old woman. If you ever had blood in your veins, it's all dried up.'

Maybe, she thought. I'm no more ignorant than you are, you big galoot, but she merely snorted and continued with her sweeping. It wasn't worth arguing with Carradine when he was in this mood. He might turn sour and, when he was sour, he could be really ugly. She had bruises on her arms and legs to prove it. Why in hell's name am I here? she wondered. I could be in High Rock or down in Mexico making good money instead of letting myself slave away for that ungenerous beast.

In the early days when Wesley Carradine was much richer from all those robberies things had been a deal better. That was when he had persuaded her and Abigail to throw in their lot with the bunch. She had known Pete Pollinger and had quite liked him at one time. A pity he had succumbed to that damned lung disease and then been caught and sent to prison. At one time she had even thought she might throw in her lot with Pete.

She stood up and shaded her eyes. 'Look over there, Wes. Someone's riding this way.'

Carradine turned and peered to where the trail was and he saw a cloud of dust with a small dot riding towards him.

It could have been Stacy or Navarro or someone riding in to claim his scalp and the reward that was attached to it.

He turned and went into the shack and came out carrying a Sharp's carbine. Now the rider was somewhat larger and more distinct and he thought, from the way he rode, that it might be Jim Stacy. A moment later he was sure.

Don't take chances, Carradine thought to himself. A man who takes chances can be shot dead. So he stood in the doorway of the cabin with the Sharp's carbine held high as the rider rode in.

It was Stacy, as he had thought, and Stacy looked none too happy as he rode in. Carradine saw immediately that were no shells in his gunbelt.

Stacy led his horse in under the shelter and offered it a drink.

Carradine lowered the carbine and stepped out into the open. 'You look like hell. Where have you been?' he asked. 'And what happened to Navarro?'

Stacy stepped on to the porch and beat his hat against his side to shake off the dust. 'Things ain't so good,' he said.

'What d'you mean, "ain't so good"?' Carradine demanded. 'Where's Navarro?'

Stacy looked away and swallowed hard. 'Navarro's dead,' he said.

'Dead? Navarro? You mean he got himself killed? How the hell did that happen?'

Stacy wondered how he could put the best gloss on what had essentially been a failure. 'There was a ruckus in town and someone tried to shoot me. That sheriff name of Steve Carrington got the drop on me and locked me up overnight and then ran me out of town.'

'Without your ammunition,' Carradine concluded, looking at the gunbelt.

Stacy grimaced. 'It ain't as bad as it sounds, Wes. I swear it ain't.'

'Then maybe you should tell me the good side and it had better be real good.'

Stacy brightened up a little. 'When we were on the edge of town, Greg Navarro shot the sheriff and someone shot Greg.' He lowered his voice. '*I think it was Pete Pollinger.*'

Carradine looked astonished. 'You *think* it was Pete Pollinger!'

'I'm pretty sure it was Pollinger.'

Carradine was trying hard to make sense of what seemed like an increasingly complicated story.

'You better come inside and fill me in on the whole situation,' he said.

Back at River Bend there was quite a furore. Doc MacFadden had bent over Greg Navarro and pronounced him dead, though there could be little doubt since there was a bullet hole right in the middle of his forehead.

'Did you shoot this man?' Mayor Shapley asked Pete Pollinger.

'I have to admit I did,' Pete Pollinger said. He was still trailing his deadly Winchester and he didn't look in the least remorseful. 'I shot him after he shot the sheriff. Least I could do. Steve Carrington was my friend and buddy. It's a pity I didn't kill this man a minute earlier. Then he wouldn't have had the chance to shoot my buddy.'

Maria was crying quietly over the body of Steve Carrington as they lifted him up gently and laid him on the stretcher the undertaker had so conveniently provided. A few minutes earlier Doc MacFadden had examined him closely as he lay face up in the dust. Navarro's bullet had hit him on the forehead and there was so much blood it was difficult to determine exactly what had happened.

After cleansing the wound, Doc MacFadden straightened up with a grim smile. 'The bullet hit him right in the forehead here,' he declared. 'Fortunately it struck at an angle and went off to the side. So it probably sliced along his skull without penetrating the brain.'

'You mean he will live?' Maria asked desperately.

'He's going have an awful bad headache,' Mayor Shapley said.

'Take him back to my place and I'll give him a closer examination,' the doctor instructed. 'And make it gentle. He's lost a lot of blood.'

They raised Steve on to the stretcher just like he was a cargo without price, and they carried him with the gentleness of doves back to the doctor's office. Maria had her hand on Steve's chest like a guardian angel as though she could scarcely believe he was still alive.

Back at High Rock the County Marshal Virgil Livermore was sitting in his office drinking the strong coffee he enjoyed when the call came through. A boy ran over from the telegraph office. 'Mr Livermore,' the boy shouted excitedly, 'a message came through from River Bend. The sheriff's been shot and they need your help.'

Marshal Livermore put on his specs (he was short sighted in his right eye, but that didn't hamper him too much; he figured he could shoot straighter with one eye closed) and read the message. He fished in his pocket and gave the boy a cent piece for his trouble. The boy spat on it and stowed it away in his jeans pocket.

Livermore went along the corridor and knocked on Judge Mann's door. The judge gave Livermore an enquiring look. 'Something on your mind, Virgil?'

'What's on my mind is this.' The marshal held out the paper. 'There seems to be trouble in River Bend, a shooting of some kind. It seems Sheriff Carrington has been shot.'

Judge Mann looked alarmed. 'You mean he's been killed?'

Virgil Livermore closed his bad eye and frowned. 'It doesn't say. It just says he's been shot, which means that, one way or the other, he must be out of action.'

Judge Mann gave a sombre nod. 'Pity,' he said. 'Steve Carrington is a real good man, one of the best. What do you aim to do?'

'Well, I think I must ride over straight away, take control. Without a sheriff River Bend might run out of control.'

'I agree,' the judge said. He read through the message again. 'River Bend is bursting at the seams,' he continued. 'There are rough elements in the place. I don't know why it's growing so fast. Something to do with the ferry, no doubt, and the cattle trade. Only one lawman and only two lockups in the calaboose. Mayor Shapley isn't going to do very much; he's too busy making a pile of money.'

'Might as well pull out now,' the marshal said. 'Be there before sundown.'

'Will you take the buggy?' the judge asked him.

'I think so. I might be there a while.'

The judge nodded. 'I might have come along with you but right now I've got my hands full.'

'Well, Deputy Marshal Rivers can fill in while I'm away,' the marshal said. 'He's young but he knows the drill.'

'Good luck,' the judge said, 'and keep me informed.'

Virgil Livermore gave him a curt salute and went out to gather his things together.

Six riders crossed the trail in front of Marshal Livermore as he drove towards River Bend. Though he was too far away to identify them, he guessed they were cow punchers from further north. But why should cow punchers be crossing the trail instead of heading along it, either in the direction of River Bend or High Rock? It didn't make sense, unless. . . . Livermore scratched the back of his neck. Unless, he thought, unless.... Right up there in the hills lay the old silver workings, played out and abandoned some years before. Could be there's somebody squatting up there, he thought. Maybe I should investigate some time.

Doc MacFadden was bending over his patient again. He placed his index finger on Steve Carrington's right eyelid and pressed down gently on the lower lid with his thumb. Then he looked closely into the sheriff's eye. The only other person in the room was Maria. She had stopped crying and stood holding her breath, waiting for the doc's verdict.

Is he going to live? she wondered.

Doc MacFadden peered even more closely into Steve Carrington's eye. 'Concussion,' he pronounced. 'He's been badly concussed but as far as I can tell his skull is intact, not even dented. He's been fortunate in that respect. There'll be a lot of bruising but we must hope for the best.'

Now that the wound had been cleaned and the bleeding had stopped, the wound was perfectly visible. Navarro's bullet had come in at a slant and cut a three inch groove through the flesh before ricocheting off to the left.

'I'm going to have to pour spirit on this and stitch this up,' the doc said, 'and hope it doesn't become infected.'

As he spoke Steve suddenly blinked and groaned. 'What?' he said and tried to struggle up from the table where they had laid him.

'Keep yourself still,' the doc said quietly. 'You're going to be OK.'

Steve blinked again. 'What the hell happened?' he asked.

'What happened was you were hit by a bullet,' the doc told him, 'but you don't need to worry. It won't happen again.' He turned to Maria who took Steve by the hand and pressed his fingers gently.

Steve's eyes fluttered open again. 'Maria,' he said quietly. 'Thank God you're here.'

'You're going to be all right,' she said. Her tears fell on his cheek.

The young woman Abigail was peering out of the window of the old silver mine cabin when she saw the approaching riders. 'Wes,' she shouted. 'We got company.'

Wesley Carradine and Jim Stacy grabbed their guns and went to the window. The older woman, Bess Woodman grabbed another gun and crouched down beside them.

'What the hell?' Carradine said. He looked out and saw six riders riding close.

The riders drew rein and stopped. One of them shouted out, 'Wesley Carradine, are you in there?'

Carradine put his finger to his lips and nobody inside the cabin spoke or coughed. Carradine peered out again and saw that the six riders were standing off and waiting.

'Wes Carradine, are you in there?' the man shouted again. 'Don't shoot, Wes. We come in peace.'

Carradine grinned. 'I know that voice. That's Finley Finn of the Pima ranch. Is that you, Finn?' he shouted.

'That's me,' the man shouted. 'Your old pal Finn. I've come with five of my buddies to make you a proposition.'

'What kind of proposition?' When a man has a price on his head he can't be too careful even with his old buddies.

85

He swung round to Jim Stacy. 'Go out there and see what they want.'

Stacy shrugged and went to the door. He felt a little nervous; after all his buddy Navarro had been shot down just a few hours back. Finley Finn was looking down at him in quite a friendly manner and Stacy knew Finn of old. They had ridden together with Wesley Carradine some years earlier when they had called themselves 'The Wild Bunch'. He recognized one or two of the other riders as well.

'The boss wants to know what you want,' Stacy said.

Finn grinned. 'Just passing by,' he said. 'Thought we'd just drop in for a friendly chat.'

'How d'you know where we were?' Wesley Carradine said from behind Stacy.

Finn shrugged. 'Didn't know where you were,' he said. 'Guess I knew where you might be. We hid out here one time before if you remember.'

Carradine did remember. Several years earlier on a stormy night with a torrent of rain lashing down a whole bunch of them had rested up here after one of the bank jobs. 'What's on your mind?' he asked suspiciously.

'Well, it's like this,' Finn said. 'Me and the boys have been laid off. No work for us to do on the ranch and a man has to earn a living somehow.'

'So what?'

'So we just walked right out of the ranch and came here. Wondered if we could come to an arrangement of some kind.'

Carradine narrowed his eyes. 'What kind would that be?'

Finn shrugged noncommittally. 'That's what we're here to discuss.'

Carradine looked over the bunch. One of them was a real old hombre with a wild beard. He looked about a

86

hundred years old, at least: a real saddle bum. 'You too, Father Time?' he said.

'Why not?' the old man croaked. 'I might be near to the end of my days but I can still hold up a gun and shoot.'

The other four waddies hooted with laughter.

'Well, you'd better come along inside,' Carradine said.

They tied their horses up in the barn and trooped into the cabin. Finn looked round appraisingly. 'Just like home,' he said. His eyes rested on Bess Woodman. 'You got the place up real good.'

'Real good,' she replied in her forthright masculine tone. 'And I hope you've brought a lot more than dust into the place.'

'Real home bird,' Father Time chortled.

The other waddies hooted again; clearly the old man was something of a character.

'Maybe introductions are in order,' Finn said. 'This here is Toby Valentine. This is Stubbs Smith. This is Chuck Cherokee. And this here is Colt Parry. I guess you've met them all, one time or another.'

Wesley Carradine ran a critical eye over the bunch. Toby Valentine looked somewhat overweight but benign. Stubbs Smith was short and square-looking. Chuck Cherokee was dark and half Indian. And Colt Parry had a hangdog look in his shifty eyes.

'What's the proposition?' Wesley Carradine asked.

'Well, like as how you got a price on your head,' Finn said, 'we thought you might care to join us and form a new *Wild Bunch.*'

Wesley Carradine looked Finn squarely in the eye; the reference to the price on his head sounded suspiciously like a threat. 'You talking about bank jobs and stages?' he asked.

Father Time decided to throw his dollar into the ring.

87

'Like this,' he said in his cracked tone. 'There's a ton of money around and we don't have it. We're as picked dry as a stiff after the buzzards have been pecking their beaks at it. This territory is rising high but we're not rising with it. So we thought we might equal the odds a little . . . and have us some fun too.'

The boys all laughed again, especially Toby Valentine.

Now everyone looked at Wesley Carradine and waited for his response.

'Like you're good with a gun and you have the brains to match,' Finn said.

Bess Woodman framed herself in the doorway. 'You boys like a little chuck to grease your innards?' she said.

Abigail carried in a huge pot and put it down on the pinewood table. 'Pitch in, boys,' she said.

Steve Carrington was now sitting in a chair and the mayor was telling him what had happened on the outskirts of town. Of course, nobody had actually witnessed the events but it wasn't difficult to put two and two together and make five and a half.

Navarro's body had been conveyed to the town mortuary where it now lay in a pinewood coffin, face up staring sight-lessly at the sky. A number of folk looked in to inspect it, especially checking the hole in its head. Among them was Juliet, the calico queen from the bordello.

She looked down at the dead man's face and sighed. 'My word,' she said. 'Who'd have thought? Just last night he was lying in bed with me. Makes one shudder to think of it, doesn't it?' Juliet had seen cadavers before but none who had been so personally involved with her.

The last visitor was Pete Pollinger who looked down at Navarro's dead face quite intently. Possibly he saw his own fate coming towards him. Yet he had no regrets; after all, if he hadn't fired the fatal shot, his buddy Steve would have been dead.

He turned to go out and met Mayor Shapley in the doorway. 'Excuse me,' the mayor said, 'but I need to ask you exactly what happened. In the absence of the sheriff I have to take charge here. That is, until the county marshal arrives.'

Pete Pollinger gave a slight bow. 'I'll be glad to be of help,' he said.

Virgil Livermore, the county marshal, drove into town in his buggy like a real caballero. He stopped at the mayor's place, took out the fat cigar he was smoking and climbed down and stretched his legs. Mayor Shapley had received a wire, so he knew the marshal was on his way. Usually, he might have left the marshal to make his own way into the office, but on this occasion he walked right out to meet him.

'Welcome, Mr Livermore,' he said. 'I see you came by buggy.' He had every reason to be pleased to see the marshal. River Bend was a growing town and might even dwarf High Rock in time. Entrepreneurs were setting up camp here as well as well-to-do lawyers and traders of one kind and another. Bordellos, too. There was even a theatre company on Main Street where they performed the latest musical pieces. All these businesses had to pay their dues to the town treasury, of which the mayor was the chairman. So any activity that would rock the metaphorical boat was frowned upon.

Marshal Livermore shook Shapley by the hand. He knew the mayor well and thought he was an up-and-coming man who might help to improve his own status in life. After all there were other things beside county marshal and the elections were due next year.

'Why don't you walk right in and I'll ask Maisie to bring you refreshments. We even have tea now, if you prefer.' The grin on the mayor's face was like the grin of the Cheshire Cat: it might easily fade away into the trees.

'Thank you kindly,' the marshal said. 'Maybe I should check in at the River Bend Hotel.'

'Very wise,' Shapley said unctuously. 'Best hotel in town. Maria does a marvellous job there. She's a real asset to the town.'

The tea was brought in and Shapley filled the marshal in on the details.

Livermore listened intently, nodding occasionally and knitting his brows. 'And the sheriff,' he asked. 'Is he going to be all right? Is he OK?'

'Well,' Shapley said egregiously, 'I believe he's conscious. Apparently the wound in his head wasn't as severe as we feared. He's in Doctor MacFadden's care at the moment. MacFadden's a wonderful doctor. Never drinks when he's on duty.'

Steve Carrington rose somewhat unsteadily to his feet.

'How do you feel?' Doc MacFadden asked him.

'Well, my head feels like it's been hit by a boulder but the mist is clearing. I think I must go back to the office and see what needs to be done.'

'You can't go back there,' Maria protested. 'You have to come to my place and rest up for a day or two.'

Steve shook his head and winced. 'I can't do that, Maria. I've got things to do.'

'But surely they can wait,' she said.

'I don't think so.' He was thinking of his buddy, Pete Pollinger, and he guessed Stacy must know Pete was in town.

In fact, Pete was standing by the door of the doc's office right now. Pete knew Steve was right. After the attempt on Steve's life and the killing of Greg Navarro, Jim Stacy had broken away. He couldn't be far and Pete had a hunch about where he might be headed.

'Give the man some peace,' the doc said. 'I can't have my patient put at risk like this. Have you ever had a crack on your skull?' For a moment he looked uncharacteristically ferocious.

Pete gave Steve a wave and walked out on to Main Street where he saw Marshal Livermore talking to the mayor. Pete knew the marshal well; in fact, Livermore had been one of the posse who had arrested him and sent him to gaol.

As he walked across Main Street Livermore turned and recognized him. The two met in the middle of Main Street and exchanged greetings. They had never been on close terms but at least they respected one another.

'Mr Pollinger,' the marshal said. 'I heard you were in town. How's your health? Where are you staying?'

'Not too far away,' Pete responded vaguely. 'I've just come from the doc's place. Been looking at my old buddy, Steve Carrington.'

The marshal nodded. 'You served in the war together, I understand.'

'Straightest guy you could ever meet,' Pete responded. 'He saved my life on more than one occasion.'

'I was just on my way over to visit with him. How is he?'

'Well, right now he has a gash on his head and a big headache. Other than that, I think he's going to be OK.'

For the first time Livermore smiled. 'I'm glad to hear that.'

'And by the way,' Pete said, 'I wanted to have a word with you, Marshal.'

The marshal's lips were still smiling but his eyes had narrowed. 'What do you want to talk to me about, Mr Pollinger?'

'Why don't we step into the River Bend Hotel; then we can take a drink together?'

Livermore did not demur. In fact he had already wired ahead to hire a room. Should I be seen drinking in a good hotel with a recently released criminal? he wondered. Yet Pollinger was an interesting character and, after all, he had served his time, hadn't he?

They ordered their drinks and sat across the table from one another. Livermore raised his glass and held it up towards Pollinger and Pollinger clinked glasses with him. It all seemed very amicable.

'Like I said, wanted to ask you something,' Pete Pollinger said.

'Ask away, my friend,' Livermore replied, sipping his drink.

Pollinger took his time. He tipped his glass and then took a long swig. 'I want you to deputize me,' he said.

CHAPTER SEVEN

'Well, let's get down to the hard brass of the matter,' Finn said.

'What would that be?' Wesley Carradine asked.

'That would be this,' Finn said. 'You want to get your hands on Pete Pollinger and find out where he stashed away that money he stole from you. We want enough gold to see us through to our old age.'

There was murmur of approval from the so-called Wild Bunch.

'I still don't get it,' Carradine said suspiciously. 'You don't need me. You could do this thing yourself.'

'That's true,' Finn agreed. 'Except for one thing.'

'And what's that?'

'That's because sooner or later someone's gonna jump you here. You can't live forever without supplies and how do you aim to get them?' He looked round at the boys, some of whom were still chuckling. Old Father Time leaned forward with his elbows on the deal table.

'They're gonna catch up on you sooner or later,' he said. 'So why don't you make it later rather than sooner?'

The Wild Bunch all leaned forward eagerly.

'Tell me what's on your mind? No ifs or buts or maybes.

Just the truth,' Wesley Carradine said.

Finn gave him a grin of satisfaction. 'Well, it's like this, Wes. We got wind of something interesting.'

'And what's that?'

'We are reliably informed there's a special delivery of gold coming through on the Fargo stage tomorrow from High Rock to River Bend, and that's one heap of gold.'

This was getting interesting. Carradine nodded. 'So?'

'I thought that might interest you,' Finn said. 'No passengers. Just the bullion.'

Old Father Time opened his mouth to speak again but Finn flapped him down. 'OK, blabber mouth, this is my call.'

This time nobody laughed.

Finn leaned forward again. 'Well, this is the deal, Wes. We take a couple of shots and bring the whole flock down. We take the bullion. Then we ride into River Bend. We pick up Pete Pollinger. You find out where he stashed your money and we have us some fun. Then we ride south across the border and live the life of the gods.'

'Will there be that much gold?' Bess Woodman asked.

'More than you could ever spend,' Finn assured her. 'Those greasers down there would welcome you with open arms . . . not that you'd want that, of course.' Finn winked at Bess Woodman.

The boys laughed again.

'Tell me more about the stage,' Wesley Carradine said.

'Not much to tell,' Finn said. 'Colt here has been in High Rock recently. He's kind of friendly with a woman up there and she works in the bank. She has sharp ears like the famous elves and she told Colt about the bullion shipment. Isn't that so, Colt?'

That man with the shifty eyes looked up from under his

hat. 'That's right,' he said.

'What about shotgun?' Wesley Carradine asked him. 'You know who will be riding shotgun?'

'Colt investigated that,' Finn said. 'Man called Brekenville. He's the usual man. Said to be a good shot but he's kind of dozy. He should be a cinch.'

Carradine was still suspicious. 'I still don't know why you want me on this?' he said.

'Like I said,' Finn explained with a wave of his hand, 'you have nothing to lose. This should hand Pete Pollinger to you on a plate. Then you can have him grilled for supper, that's if he's still alive.'

Old Father Time pitched in again. 'Pollinger has the consumption right up to here.' He put his hand across his throat. 'We don't get there quick, he's likely to drop dead of the fever anyway.'

There was more laughter which didn't improve Carradine's temper. The old geek was beginning to grate on his nerves.

'So you want me to deputize you?' Marshal Livermore held up his glass and peered at Pete Pollinger from behind it. 'Tell me why I should do that, Mr Pollinger?'

Pete Pollinger was smiling to himself. 'One reason is I know where Wesley Carradine is holed up and I can take you there.'

Marshal Livermore's raised his eyebrows. 'You know where Carradine is holed up?' he said with some surprise.

Pollinger nodded. 'As you know, there's a price on Carradine's head, only five hundred dollars, I believe, but that's something.'

Livermore put his head on one side and listened.

'Not only that, marshal. There's an election coming up

soon and bringing in Carradine, dead or alive, could give you some benefit. . . .'

Livermore's eyes narrowed. He had never known Pollinger intimately but now he was beginning to appreciate the quality of his mind.

'And another thing,' Pete Pollinger said. 'I'm good with a gun. A man who is good with a gun could be useful when it comes to digging out Wesley Carradine, especially if you want to reap the benefits I just mentioned.'

Steve Carrington was just entering the River Bend Hotel with the owner Maria when he looked over and saw his friend Pete Pollinger sitting with Marshal Livermore drinking beer. The sheriff had his head bandaged at a slant so that he looked like a clown peering out of one eye.

'That's Pete chatting to the county marshal,' he said. 'Or has the gash on my head affected my eyesight?'

Maria was looking concerned. But she smiled. The bullet might have knocked him out cold but it hadn't dented his sense of humour.

They went over to the table and the two drinkers looked up at them. Marshal Livermore stood up to greet them. He fancied himself as a gentleman. 'Why, Maria,' he said, 'it's great to see you again. You look younger and more beautiful every day.'

Pete Pollinger remained seated. He had never claimed to be anything more than a gunslinger with tuberculosis. He was looking directly at his old friend the sheriff. 'How's your head doing?' he asked.

'Well, it still seems to be on my neck unless I'm dreaming,' Steve told him. 'But I could do with a drink.'

They sat down at the table and Marshal Livermore ordered beers all round. Maria decided to sit it out; she was still concerned about Steve's head. A man with concussion might be more injured than he knew.

When she had gone off, ostensibly to talk to a member of her staff, Marshal Livermore offered Steve and Pete cigars but both declined. Pete no longer smoked because of his sickness. Steve had never smoked because he cared too much for his health and why would a man with a hole in his head start smoking, anyway?

'I've come to a decision,' Livermore said portentously. 'Since you're indisposed at the moment, sheriff, I've decided to deputize Pete here.'

Steve wrinkled his brow and looked at Pete. 'Is that so?' he said with an air of nonchalance.

Pete nodded. 'I figured I could be useful.' He winked at Steve.

'Of course,' Livermore added. 'I'd need to talk to my old friend the mayor about it and consult the judge, but I don't think they're likely to raise any objection, especially because it might help me to bring Wesley Carradine to justice, and that's what we all want, isn't it?'

For some reason that made Pete laugh and his laugh led to a fit of coughing and to blood on his kerchief.

Steve watched with concern. A fat cigar-smoking marshal, a sheriff with a hole in his head, and a man dying of the consumption. What a posse, he thought.

'Like we do it this way,' Wesley Carradine said as the Wild Bunch crowded round. He dipped his finger in his beer and drew a line on the deal table. 'This is the arroyo, the best place to hold up the stage.' He jabbed his finger down on the side of what marked the trail. 'Up here among the rocks is the best place. You can see the stage coming for miles. You, Finn, will ride down in front to head it off. You take Father Time, and Colt Parry and the rest of us come up behind the coach. There shouldn't be any kind of a problem if we do it well.'

'After that, what then?' Colt Parry asked.

'After that we make for the border,' Finn said.

'Not quite,' Wesley Carradine said. 'After that we ride into River Bend and burn the place down.' He looked round triumphantly and the whole bunch grew silent. Could they believe their ears?

'Burn the place down?' Stubbs Smith said breathlessly.

'Why not?' Wesley Carradine replied. 'The whole place is no more than a nest of rattlesnakes with rats sneaking through the streets and crawling under every building. It deserves to go to Perdition.'

'I didn't know that was part of the deal,' Toby Valentine said. 'Nobody said anything about burning the place down.'

Then Father Time pitched in again. 'I like a damned good fire,' he said enthusiastically. 'There's a kind of justice in that. I think you got it just about right.'

Most of the boys laughed but, perhaps, a little less enthusiastically than before. Burning a whole town down was, to say the least, somewhat ambitious.

'How are we gonna do it?' Toby Valentine asked.

'No problem with that,' Carradine said. 'The whole place is just a pile of wooden shacks. It'll blaze away like the hobs of Hell.'

After a moment Jim Stacy piped up. 'What about Pete Pollinger? How do we get even with him?'

Wesley Carradine grinned. 'I've been thinking about that so you don't need to worry too much. If my plan works out you'll see Pollinger swinging from a beam with flames coming out of every orifice in his body.

Now the boys laughed somewhat more boisterously.

When Wesley Carradine was in full flow he could paint a lively picture. He was a real artist.

While the boys were laughing and drinking Bess Woodman and Abigail Winter were outside rustling up another meal with what ingredients they could muster. Supplies were getting short and Bess was worried. Soon someone would have to ride into town and buy or steal flour and meat. Men didn't think of that kind of thing. All they wanted to do was stalk around like cockerels, crowing and firing their guns off. She had fallen in with Wesley Carradine some years back and she had been loyal all through the difficult times. Bess had had a hard life. Her father had been a drunken bully and her mother a woman of the streets. She had seen Wesley Carradine as a man on the way up who would one day be rich. She dreamed of a neat little farm somewhere where they could settle down together and look after a few hens and maybe some sheep and pigs. When she heard Carradine boasting about burning River Bend down she was alarmed. It reminded her of her father in one of his uglier moods. She thought Wes had gone off his head.

Abigail was alarmed too. When she heard Carradine talking about burning the town down she felt the flames scorching her very soul. But she was even more worried about Pete Pollinger whom she had once met and whom she still remembered fondly. She knew he had done time in gaol and she also knew he was desperately sick, and something inside her reached out to him.

'You hear what those galoots are saying?' Bess said to her behind the door.

'D'you think he means that about burning River Bend to the ground?' Abigail asked her.

Bess shrugged her ample shoulders. 'Wes always boasts

when he's drunk,' she said. 'He likes to impress other men. Particularly men like Finn. You ask me, that Finn is a terrible hombre. He likes to stir things up but, when the time comes, he's gonna let you down.'

'What about Pete Pollinger?' Abigail asked quietly. 'D'you think he really stole that money from Wes?'

'Of course!' Bess said. 'But that doesn't matter nohow. What matters is that Wes is really burning himself up for revenge.'

'What d'you think we should do, Bess?' Abigail asked her.

'What we do, girl, is we stick together,' Bess said. 'We look after one another in this, we're gonna come up swimming. So, when the time comes, we got to break out of this situation and make sure we survive. That's the main thing.'

The two women looked at one another intently for a moment and then gave one another a high five.

Next morning, just after sunrise, the special Wells Fargo coach pulled out of High Rock with its load of bullion. The Fargo agent had checked everything out and the driver, Sam Holtby, signed for the bullion box. Then the two men riding shotgun signed. On routine trips there was only one man riding shotgun but on this occasion there were to be two. One would perch up there with the driver, Sam. The other would be riding in the cab, sitting on the bullion. The man perching next to the driver was Jake Brekenville, one of the most experienced of the Wells Fargo guards. The other, younger less-experienced guard John Gullimore, sat in the cab nursing a shotgun and a Winchester rifle. Though young, Gullimore had a reputation as a steady hand and a reliable man with a gun.

The Fargo agent shook hands with the three men in turn. 'Now you boys, have a safe ride to River Bend and deliver the gold to the authorities there. The county marshal will be waiting at the station and the chief bank teller will be waiting to sign it in. You understand me, boys?'

The three men murmured their assent. Everyone knew that the agent was full of gas but they tolerated him because he was the boss.

'Now boys,' he said, 'have a good steady drive and don't stop to talk to any strange men on the way, you hear me?'

The driver and the two guards gave a growl of laughter and Sam Holtby whipped up the horses and pulled away.

Marshal Livermore had just received news that the Fargo stage was on its way from High Rock. He and the Sheriff Steve Carrington and Pete Pollinger were about to saddle up and ride out in search of Wesley Carradine and his bunch. Pete Pollinger had assured Marshal Livermore that he had a hunch where Wesley Carradine was holed up and the county marshal was anxious to make the arrest and claim the reward. It would also boost his chances of winning the next election for county marshal and might even enhance his business opportunities.

'Before we ride out,' he said to Pete Pollinger, 'how many men are in the Carradine outfit?'

'Well, we know there's Jim Stacy and there would have been Navarro if we hadn't shot him dead,' Pete Pollinger said. 'Nobody else as far as I know.'

'OK.' Livermore took out his fat cigar and puffed aromatic smoke into the air. 'Now you've been deputized maybe you could tell us where Carradine is holed up. That way, if anything happens to you on the way, we know where we're going.'

Steve Carrington thought that was no way to treat his old buddy, but he didn't say anything. He thought he might

101

know the answer, anyway.

'Well, I don't promise anything,' Pete said, 'but my guess is they're holed out up at the old silver workings some-where.'

Marshal Livermore held up his cigar with something like glee. 'That means we can ride up there and take them by surprise. Pity you didn't tell us about that before, Mr Pollinger.'

Steve nodded.

But before they could ride out the message about the Fargo stage came through.

When Mayor Shapley heard the news he jumped on his horse and rode down to the Well Fargo office where the three officers of the law were sitting on their horses.

'The boy from the telegraph office has just run across with the news; the bullion stage is on its way. What are you going to do?'

Marshal Livermore smiled and waved his half smoked cigar at him. 'Well, Mayor, what we aim to do is to ride out and apprehend that renegade Wesley Carradine. That's what we aim to do.'

'How come?' the mayor enquired.

'How come is my new deputy knows where he's at.'

Pete Pollinger turned to exchange glances with Steve Carrington.

Mayor Shapley frowned. 'In that case, gentlemen, I think I should ride with you. It's my job as mayor to protect this town and look after its citizens. I could take the day off and make sure Carradine and his henchmen are brought to justice.'

Steve looked across at him and smiled. 'Can you fire a gun without killing yourself?' he asked.

Shapley looked deeply offended. 'If I may remind you, Sheriff, I am in charge of this town and, when you were in trouble with those men who wanted to hang that foolish young desperado who tried to hold up the River Bend Hotel it was me who stepped in to help you.'

'You certainly did, Mr Mayor.' Steve doffed his hat.

Finley Finn was on his horse looking down at the trail that curved away towards High Rock. With him were Old Father Time and Colt Parry.

There was an excellent view from up there towards High River. Finn took a spy glass from his saddle-bag and focused on the trail.

'Wes chose well,' Finn said. 'We must give him that. He may be a bit rusty in the joints but he knows his stuff.'

'He's more than a bit rusty; he's falling to bits,' Old Father Time said.

Finn gave him a sneer. 'Wesley Carradine could beat you to the draw any day,' he said.

Old Father Time laughed. 'Beating a man to the draw doesn't mean a thing. It's shooting straight that counts.'

'Well, you might have a chance to prove it soon,' said Colt Parry with a sly grin.

'Like in the next twenty minutes,' Finn said, 'because I can see the stage coming right now, dead on time too.' He handed Old Father Time the spyglass and the old man peered out along the trail.

'Looks kind of like a toy,' the old man said. 'A toy with six horses. They usually have but four.'

'Not when they're carrying bullion. With bullion you have to have six for speed,' Finn said.

'That's a fact,' Colt Parry agreed.

*

103

Just about the time that Finn sat looking down at the approaching coach, a small group of monks were setting out from the Jesuit House to ride down to River Bend in order to purchase supplies for the brothers. Leading them in the buggy was Father Sylvester and, beside him, was Eleazer Stebbins, the young man who had tried to hold up the River Bend Hotel unsuccessfully. But this was an entirely different Stebbins. His head had been shaved clean and he looked like a monk himself. In fact, shortly after being admitted to the Jesuit House, he had asked for an audience with Father Sylvester who had him shown into the room which was more of a cell than a study.

'Now, Eleazer,' the good father said. 'I hear you are quite restless but you have done well and I think you'll soon be ready to go out into the world again.' Father Sylvester gave him a benign smile and a blessing.

Eleazer wasn't good with words but he knew he had something important to say. 'I don't know as how I'm ready to go out into the world yet,' he stammered. 'You've been right good to me here and I think I'd like to stay and maybe become . . .' He paused and waved his arms, struggling to find the right words.

Father Sylvester held up his hand again. 'I understand,' he said, 'but I think it's a little too early to think about that. You've worked hard here and we all appreciate that, but these decisions are not made lightly and first we must be sure you have a vocation.'

Eleazor had little notion what vocation meant but he said, 'What must I do?'

'You must work and pray,' Father Sylvester told him. 'Work and pray, my son.'

Father Sylvester wasn't surprised by the boy's decision. He had grown quite fond of Eleazer and thought that someday he might become a novice and even join the order, except that he lacked *real* mental capacity.

That was why Eleazer Stebbins was sitting on the buckboard with Father Sylvester and the two other monks.

As they approached the trail leading to River Bend, Eleazer looked to the right and spotted the Fargo coach.

'Why look, Father, there's a coach on the trail.'

'Yes, I see it,' Father Sylvester said.

As he spoke, something quite surprising happened. Five riders rode into the draw ahead of them and they were all wearing bandannas to conceal their lower faces.

'My God, there's going to be a hold-up!' Eleazer Stebbins declared with horror.

Father Sylvester stared calmly at the hold-up men. It took a great deal to throw him off course. The other two monks exchanged uneasy glances. But it was already too late to warn the Fargo coach of the danger. The hold-up men had spotted the monks, and, as three of them rode on, two of them turned and rode back towards them.

Chuck Cherokee pointed a Winchester carbine at Father Sylvester and ordered the monks to rein in the horses. Eleazer Stebbins was at the reins and he did as he was bid.

'What's going on here?' Stebbins demanded.

'That's none of your business,' Chuck Cherokee said. 'You just do as I say and nobody's gonna get hurt.'

The Wells Fargo coach was bumping along quite happily when Jake Brekenville, who was riding shotgun, saw the three riders riding down the draw towards them. They were wearing bandannas to cover their faces too.

'Aha, I think we got a situation here,' he said to Sam Holtby, the driver.

'What do we do?' Jake Brekenville said in alarm.

'It depends,' Sam muttered between his teeth. He had faced attempted holdups before; so he had some experience. 'We could either stop and let them take us or we could push forward and ride them down.' He knew that with six reasonably fresh horses he might outrun the robbers and get away, especially with Jake Brekenville gunning at them with his Winchester.

At that moment the other shotgun, John Gullimore, was peering out of the back of the coach. 'There's riders coming up on us from behind!' he shouted.

Sam Holtby was no cinch. He had driven Fargo coaches for twenty years and had even been awarded a company medal for good service. 'Tell you what we do,' he said to Jake Brekenville. 'I'm gonna whip the team up and you can lie flat and shoot at those bastards. I aim to get through to River Bend, come hell or high water.'

As Brekenville scrambled back and lay prone on top of the coach Sam urged the horses forward into a full gallop.

Bess Woodman and Abigail Winter were still in the old silver mine cabin, getting their things together ready to move out. Wesley had given them orders to ride to a place overlooking the Pima Ranch where the whole bunch would assemble and ride down to the border. Only, Bess and Abigail had other plans. Both were sick and tired of Wesley Carradine's bullying ways and wanted to be free of him, especially now that Finley Finn had turned up with his so-called *Wild Bunch.* Who were they kidding, anyway?

'What do we do?' Abigail asked the older woman.

Bess Woodman put on a brave face but she didn't know the answer to that question. They could ride down to Mexico and strike out on their own or they could ride east to Texas and start afresh somewhere there. They could even ride west to California where their chances might be even better.

But fate had other things in mind for them. As they were getting their meagre belongings together they heard a shot.

'Come out with your hands up!' someone shouted. 'Any shooting and you get killed!'

Bess had grabbed her Sharps and she crouched by the window ready to fire. When she peered out cautiously she saw two men with rifles. One was Steve Carrington and the other was Pete Pollinger.

Steve Carrington dropped down on one knee and got ready to fire another shot. Pete Pollinger levelled his gun at the window.

Bess Woodman hesitated for no more than two seconds. 'Don't fire,' she called out. 'There's just two of us women in here.'

'That's encouraging to hear,' Steve shouted back. 'Now you just come to the door and throw down your guns. You can't get away so you might as well give up. We're not keen on bloodshed here. If there are any menfolk in there tell them to come out first. We've got the place boxed in. So that's the best thing you can do.'

Finley Finn was surprised when he saw the Fargo coach was being drawn by six horses. But he was even more amazed when he realized that the driver had no intention of stopping. In fact, Sam Holtby was lashing the horses and giving an unearthly yell as he urged his team into a full gallop. The Fargo agent had selected the horses well and Sam Holtby hadn't pressed them hard. So they responded well.

As Finn rode ahead of the coach he pulled his horse round to avoid a collision. He had intended to fire a warning shot from his Winchester carbine but he couldn't bring it round in time. He saw Jake Brekenville peering at him as the coach flashed by and he heard the crash as Brekenville fired his Winchester.

Goddammit, he thought as he fired his own Winchester.

Firing from the top of a juddering coach or from a veering horse is notoriously difficult. So both bullets missed by a yard!

Breckenville's blood was up and he was laughing. 'Keep going, Sam!' he said between his teeth as he levered his carbine and sucked in his breath for a second shot.

Finn had dropped away and now Toby Valentine was galloping in somewhat faster than one might have expected from such a heavy man. Brekenville half turned and took a bead on the rider and fired, and Toby Valentine reared up and dropped behind his terrified horse.

'That's one down,' Brekenville muttered to himself, levering his carbine again. Then he saw the figure of doom on the hill just above him. Old Father Time might have looked like a freaky old geek but he knew what he was doing. He had reined in his horse and was standing back in the stirrups taking aim at the coach. As he squeezed the trigger, he had the pleasure of seeing Brekenville's head jerk sideways before he slid off the top of the coach and rolled away over the side.

Old Father Time was trying to think of something funny but at that moment John Gullimore poked his shotgun out of the coach window and let fly at the old man. Old Father Time was still laughing when he took the whole load of buckshot full in the face and his dreams of fame ended with a splatter of blood and brains.

Wesley Carradine and Jim Stacy were riding hard in pursuit of the coach, closely followed by Stubbs Smith. They saw

Old Father Time rear back with blood pouring from his face and Toby Valentine lying groaning and dying on the trail with the body of Jake Brekenville not too far ahead.

Finn had dismounted and he was taking aim and firing systematically at the rapidly disappearing coach.

'Well, that's one big damned failure!' Wesley Carradine shouted to Jim Stacy as though it were his fault.

'We can still stop the coach,' Stubbs Smith said breathlessly. 'Those horses can't gallop like that all the way to River Bend. We keep going we can still get that gold. If we take out the lead horses the whole team is gonna have to stop.'

Finley Finn had thought of that too. He swung quickly into the saddle again and galloped on to head off the coach.

Chuck Cherokee was pointing his rifle at Father Sylvester, and Colt Parry was looking somewhat nervously along the trail in the direction of the attempted hold-up.

'Get down off that buggy!' Chuck Cherokee ordered.

'Do as he says,' Father Sylvester said to the monks. The two monks and Father Sylvester clambered down from the buggy but Eleazer Stebbins hesitated.

'You too, bald head!' Chuck Cherokee waved the rifle at him.

'It ain't no use holding us up. We ain't got nothing to give you,' Stebbins said.

Chuck Cherokee walked right up to Eleazer Stebbins and jabbed the barrel of the rifle against his head. 'One more word and I'll blow a hole clean through that bald pate of yourn!'

'Do as the man says, Eleazer,' Father Sylvester said quietly.

Eleazer's face had turned as yellow as cream. He stepped down from the buggy with shaking legs.

'Now, put your hands in the air,' Chuck Cherokee ordered. The monks raised their hands above their heads.

'As Eleazer says we have nothing to offer,' Father Sylvester said.

Chuck Cherokee grinned. He had no love of priests or monks or any sort of Holy Joes. In fact, he despised them. To him they were just plain vermin. 'Now, you just get down on your knees and swallow a mouthful of dust,' he said. '*Dust to dust, ashes to ashes.*'

He laughed.

CHAPTER EIGHT

Up at the old silver mine workings Bess Woodman was considering her options. She had been with Wesley Carradine for several years and had thought he was a good bet, but now things had changed and she reckoned Carradine's fortunes had taken a sharp turn for the worse. This was largely because of the arrival of Finley Finn who was, she thought, a malign influence.

In this male dominated world, a woman had to consider her position and use her wits, and Bess had become quite adept at that. After all her years of poverty, neglect, and abuse Bess still had the yearning for a good comfortable home and a husband who would provide for her. If the right man showed up, she might even have a family, too. In the meantime she had Abigail who was almost as good as a daughter to her. Though Abigail was none too bright, she had an even temperament and liked to please.

Bess was trying to work things out when Steve Carrington and Pete Pollinger arrived on the scene. She knew Pete Pollinger had been sick, but he had a lot of grit and, if it hadn't been for the illness she might have fancied him as a partner. Now she saw that he was emaciated almost to the point of cadaverousness and his skin had a parchment yellowness about it, though his eyes gleamed with a kind of devilish liveliness.

She didn't know Steve Carrington but guessed from the badge that he was some kind of law officer. She also saw that he had a large bandage above his ear.

'You been injured, sheriff?' she asked him directly.

Steve grinned. 'Had a slight collision with a bullet,' he said. 'Fortunately my skull proved too thick. So it bounced off.'

'The *hombre* who fired that shot was a friend of yours,' Pete Pollinger said. 'Name of Navarro. It was the last shot he ever fired.'

'What happened to him?' Abigail asked.

'I guess I had to shoot him,' Pete said. 'He's stretched out in a pinewood coffin at the funeral directors down in River Bend.'

Abigail gasped.

Pete gave a sardonic grin. 'Sorry to be the bearer of bad news, miss.'

'Where's Wesley Carradine?' Steve asked the two women.

Before they could reply there was clatter outside and Marshal Livermore and Mayor Shapley showed up with their guns drawn somewhat over-dramatically.

Bess knew Livermore since she frequently rode into High Rock for supplies. She had always considered him something of a fat slob with his swanky cigars and his air of self-importance. In fact, even here, he had the stub of a cigar stuck in the corner of his mouth.

'Well, well, well,' the marshal said. 'I didn't think to see such a fine lady up at the old silver workings.' He took out the cigar stub and wagged his head at her. 'Seems you've fallen into bad company, madam.'

Bess was still considering her options. It was obvious that Wesley Carradine's cover had been blown. What could she do to get the best out of the situation? She saw out of the corner of her eye that Abigail was shaking with fear and would probably break at any moment.

Mayor Shapley spoke for the first time. 'If Carradine's been here,' he said, 'he can't be far off. So you'd better spill the beans. There is a reward, you know.'

Bess was still considering matters when Abigail broke. 'We're just slaves,' she whined. 'We don't mean no harm. We just keep house here as far as we can.'

'In that case why were you loading up ready to pull out?' Steve asked her.

'That's because we decided we couldn't take any more abuse,' Bess said. 'We're going to go away from here and look for a better life.'

'That sounds reasonable,' Steve said. 'Then I guess we arrived in time to save you before Wesley Carradine gets back.' He was smiling quite benignly below the bandage.

Abigail was struggling to speak and at last it came out. 'They're gonna burn the town down!' she blurted out. 'That's why we're leaving because it's such a bad thing to do!'

'Burn the town down!' Mayor Shapley said aghast. 'Which town?'

'And they're holding up the stage, too!' Abigail cried out.

Marshal Livermore decided it was time to take control. He took out his cigar stub and hurled it to the ground. 'Now, ladies, I think it's time to come clean and tell us the whole deal.'

That was when the story came tumbling out, including the arrival of Finley Finn and *The Wild Bunch*, the planned attack on the stage, and the intended burning down of River Bend.

Sam Holtby was still lashing the stage coach horses when the lead horse went lame and the whole outfit came to a slithering halt. They were no more than a mile from River Bend.

'What the hell!' Holtby shouted in frustration.

The coach had slid to one side and careened to a halt.

'What's going on?' John Gullimore asked as he emerged from the cabin.

'What's going on is we got a lame horse and it's broken its leg.' Holtby leaped down from the cabin and went forward to investigate. He saw at once that what he had feared was true: one of the lead horses was kicking out feebly and whinnying with agony. There was only one solution; he must shoot the horse and cut it free. Then maybe they could limp on to River Bend.

John Gullimore was looking back along the trail. 'No time for that, Sam. We got company,' he said.

Indeed, they had got company. Stubbs Smith was less than half a mile away and was riding hell for leather towards them. Behind him, not too far off, were Wesley Carradine and Jim Stacy. Up on the hill to the left Finley Finn was aiming his Winchester again.

'We got two possibilities,' Sam said between tight lips. 'We can take cover behind the coach and shoot it out or we can run for the rocks up there and save our skins.'

'Never turn your back on a man with a gun,' John Gullimore said. 'We got to stay and shoot it out.'

Eleazer Stebbins was bowing down to the earth with the two monks and Father Sylvester. There was a smell of death in the air and he sensed that Chuck Cherokee might not be squeamish about firing his Winchester. In the weeks Eleazer had been at the Jesuit House he had become deeply attached to Father Sylvester and thought he was just about the best man he had ever known.

'You the boss of this outfit?' Chuck Cherokee shouted, prodding Father Sylvester in the back of the neck with his Winchester.

Father Sylvester wasn't easily cowed. 'We don't have bosses,' he said bravely from the ground. 'But I'm the ordained priest, if that's what you mean.'

Chuck Cherokee gave him a vicious poke in the back of the head. 'Don't be funny with me!' he snarled as Father Sylvester pitched forward with a grunt of pain.

Eleazer Stebbins was seized by a sudden fit of rage. He had noticed that Colt Parry had remounted his horse and ridden on, leaving Chuck Cherokee alone with the prisoners. Chuck Cherokee was now moving among the monks, prodding and bashing at their heads with his Winchester. 'You damned bald-headed coots!' he raved. Then he started kicking out at them like a madman.

Eleazer couldn't stand it anymore. He was young and agile and hot headed and, as Chuck Cherokee kicked out at the monk nearest to him, Eleazer suddenly caught at his foot and wrenched it to one side. Cherokee was thrown completely off balance and he fired his Winchester as he fell on his back. The bullet lodged in the side of the buckboard and the monks cried out in alarm.

Eleazer Stebbins was no pugilist but he was on his feet in a flash, kicking out at Chuck Cherokee. One of his blows caught Cherokee on the side of the head and sent him sprawling on to his side.

Father Sylvester leaped up with surprising speed and he

snatched at the Winchester and he wrenched it away from Cherokee.

Now Cherokee was sliding backwards, reaching for his side arm, but Eleazer drove his heel into the man's midriff. The monks swarmed over Cherokee and Eleazer snatched the pistol from its holster and cocked it.

'Enough!' shouted Father Sylvester. 'No more violence in God's name!'

The monks drew back, winded and terrified and Eleazer covered Chuck Cherokee with the revolver. 'Get up and put your hands in the air!' he commanded.

Chuck Cherokee got to his feet with some difficulty and raised his hands.

Steve Carrington, Pete Pollinger and the rest of them, including Bess and Abigail, were riding towards the trail from High Rock to River Bend when they heard the shooting. Steve held up his arm and they all came to a sudden halt. 'That must be the stage,' he said.

'That's like I told you,' Bess Woodman said. She was now doing her damned best to ingratiate herself with the lawmen.

Pete Pollinger gave a growl of anger. 'We got to get down there and save the coach,' he said.

'Damned the coach. What about the gold?' the mayor said.

They jigged their horses and rode towards the trail, and the first thing they came across was the monks and Chuck Cherokee with his hands raised above his head. Eleazer Stebbins still had Cherokee's pistol in his hand.

'Well, boy, I see you rose to the occasion this time,' Steve said. 'I think maybe you should give me the gun.'

Stebbins handed over the pistol without demur.

'Where's the stage?' Pete Pollinger asked.

'Just a little way along the trail,' Father Sylvester told them breathlessly. 'We've got to do something to stop the killing.'

Sam Holtby and John Gullimore were crouching behind the coach as Stubbs Smith rode up wearing the bandanna to cover his lower face.

'Stand-off!' Sam shouted as he peered round the corner of the coach.

'Stand-off, be damned!' Stubbs Smith shouted. 'Why don't you boys just run for cover while you can? We ain't interested in you. We just want that box of bullion you got on board.' He levelled his Colt and fired off a round.

Sam Holtby dodged behind the coach and John Gullimore fired at Stubbs Smith with his Winchester.

Sam looked back along the trail and saw Colt Parry and Wesley Carradine, closely followed by Jim Stacy. And on the bluff above them Finley Finn was aiming his Winchester for another shot. 'We ain't got a chance of a snowball in hell!' he said to Gullimore.

At that moment Finley Finn fired his Winchester and John Gullimore never knew what hit him. The bullet struck him full on the temple and mashed his brains.

Sam Holtby gasped with horror and threw down his gun. 'Don't fire!' he pleaded.

Finley Finn and Wesley Carradine rode in with their guns levelled. Sam Holtby looked down at John Gullimore's twitching body and was violently sick. 'For God's sake don't shoot!' he cried again.

Finley Finn was laughing. 'You gotta go sometime,' he said. 'Now just stand with your hands held high and you might just about survive.'

117

Wesley Carradine and Stubbs Smith were already inside the coach, hauling out the box of bullion. 'My God, this bullion sure is heavy!' Stubbs Smith laughed. 'Enough to sink a battleship.'

'Or keep us in clover for the rest of our lives,' Wesley Carradine said.

'What do we do now?' Stubbs Smith asked him.

Wesley Carradine looked down at the strong box and pondered. 'What we do is we use the team to haul it off the trail. That's no problem.'

But there was a problem. Where would they take the bullion and how would they share it out? Nobody seemed to have thought of that.

Steve Carrington and Pete Pollinger heard the shots and judged them to be no more than a mile up the trail close to River Bend. Mayor Shapley and Marshal Livermore were alarmed.

Shapley said, 'We've got to save that gold! River Bend depends on it!'

'What do you suggest?' Marshal Livermore asked.

'You take charge of the prisoner,' Steve suggested to Livermore. 'Keep him in custody until we sort this whole thing out.'

'Good idea,' Mayor Shapley said in approval.

Chuck Cherokee had his hands tied behind his back and he was fuming with rage. Why had he been such a damned fool when he could have been in on the robbery?

Steve and Pete were already spurring their horses along the trail towards River Bend.

Father Sylvester, the two monks and Eleazer Stebbins were also in a quandary. The two monks were somewhat jittery and the women seemed undecided about what to do next.

'What are we going to do?' Abigail asked Bess quietly.

'We keep calm and work things out,' Bess advised. She felt decidedly uneasy when she met Father Sylvester's relentless gaze.

Marshal Livermore had no such qualms. In fact, he was relieved that, for him, the fighting was over. So he took out his cigar case and offered them round, except to the prisoner. Father Sylvester and the monks politely declined but, to his surprise, Bess Woodman accepted.

'I didn't know women folk smoked cigars,' Eleazer said in amazement.

'I smoke everything,' Bess said proudly.

'I've got a better idea,' Wesley Carradine said.

'What d'you suggest?' Finn asked him suspiciously. He was thinking about how they could share out the gold and how he and the boys deserved the biggest bite since it had been his idea in the first place. He might even keep the lot for himself if he played his cards right.

'What we do,' Carradine said, 'is we unharness that lame critter and ride on through the town and out the other side. A mile out there's South Fork and we can go right on down to Mexico that way.'

'But how can we take this rig down to Mexico?' Stubbs Smith objected.

Jim Stacy gave a nervous snigger. 'You got a point there, Stubbs.'

'We don't do that,' Carradine said. 'What we do is we pick up a buggy in town, load the gold on board, and ride on to South Fork.

'As easy as that?' Stubbs Smith said sarcastically.

'It's the only way,' Carradine said. 'We can't go back and

we can't go off the trail with this rig. River Bend won't know what hit it.'

'I think you're probably right,' Finley Finn piped up. 'Get that lame horse out of harness just as quick as you can. And you' – he motioned at Sam Holtby with his Winchester – 'when you finish messing your pants, you get your arse up there in the driving-seat and whip up the horses, you hear me?'

Sam Holtby lost no time in scrambling up on to the driving-seat. A minute before he had expected to be dead like John Gulliver and Jake Brekenville and now he realized he might live a little longer if he kept his wits.

Stubbs Smith and Colt Parry rapidly released the injured horse from its traces.

'Think we should put the critter out of its misery?' Colt Parry said.

'No time for that,' Wesley Carradine said, 'and no need to waste bullets. You might need it later to blow out your brains if this goes wrong.'

Stubbs Smith got up next to Sam Holtby to make sure he didn't try any tricks and they all mounted up and rode on towards River Bend.

It wasn't long before Steve Carrington and Pete Pollinger found the bodies lying beside the trail. It was like a battle-field strewn with corpses, pretty ghastly ones too! Toby Valentine looked like a bloated whale, Father Time had hardly anything left of his face, Jake Breckenville had his head in a cactus plant and, further on, John Gullimore lay with a bloody dent in his head. It was a gruesome collection but neither of the two hardened warriors was sick. They had both seen worse in the war.

Steve said, 'I know it's crazy but I do believe those killers are riding on to River Bend. We might even catch up on them before they get there.'

His old buddy Pete Pollinger was less optimistic. 'If I know Carradine he's intent on more killing. Probably thinks I'm waiting for him there. One thing to our advantage is he doesn't know we're right behind him.'

'Well, we don't know how many of them there are,' Steve said.

Pete leaned over and inspected the tracks. 'We have a good idea. These are the coach tracks and right here are the tracks of the riders. Difficult to tell but I reckon there must be at least four of them, maybe five.'

'That's two against five,' Steve said. 'We'd better ride fast.'

Marshal Livermore was smoking his cigar when the two women made their break. It wasn't the best smoke he had ever had but at least it calmed his frayed nerves a little.

'Thanks for the cigar,' Bess said, holding out the half-finished cigar towards him.

Livermore smiled and nodded. He prided himself that he had a way with the ladies. 'You're welcome, dear madam,' he said with a gracious bow.

The next second Bess had hurled the half-smoked cigar in his face. Mayor Shapley stared in amazement as the marshal recoiled and the two women swung their horses round and spurred them away.

'What the hell!' Mayor Shapley pulled his gun but didn't cock it.

'See you in Amarillo!' Bess shouted over her shoulder as they galloped away.

'See you in Amarillo!' Abigail echoed.

'Why don't you shoot them down?' Chuck Cherokee

sneered. 'They're only women. Ain't you big enough for that, Marshal?'

'No more violence!' Father Sylvester said.

'Shut your mouth!' Eleazer shouted, raising his fist at Chuck Cherokee.

Bess and Abigail were both good riders and they were quickly out of earshot of the party round Father Sylvester's buck-board.

'What do we actually aim to do?' Abigail asked Bess.

'Don't you worry your little head about that,' Bess said. 'We got supplies, don't we?'

'Are we really riding to Amarillo?'

'Amarillo, Mexico, anywhere you like. Just as long as we get away from these stupid men.'

'But suppose we meet bad men on the trail, how can we protect ourselves. We ain't even armed.'

'You don't have to worry about that, baby.' Bess reached into her saddle-bag and produced a .32 calibre Smith & Wesson revolver. 'Any man who wants to molest us will have to deal with this little number.'

Bess laughed and the two women rode on.

Frederick Yango, the portly Wells Fargo agent was pacing up and down outside the office, peering at his gold fob watch through his rather minute and unreliable spectacles. He had had a wire through from the main office in High Rock that the stage was on its way, but it was now at least an hour late and he was worried.

There weren't many people around since this was an irregular coach with gold on board and there wouldn't be anyone special to greet. Among the few who were waiting were the bank manager and a teller and the somewhat for-midable figure of Brig Bailey who had wanted to see Eleazer

Stebbins swing after the attempted hold-up at the River Bend Hotel. Brig now had a Colt revolver stuck through his belt.

'What d'you think's happening out there, Fred?' Brig asked in his usual gruff tone.

Frederick Yango peered at him through his pebble glasses with a worried look on his rotund face. 'I don't know, Brig. All I can say is that coach should have arrived more than an hour back.'

'You know how many guards they have on board?'

'I'm told there are two and the driver, of course.'

'That would be Sam Holtby, I guess,' Brig said. 'I know him well. Most reliable driver of the lot, but . . .' Brig stroked his moustache. He was a rising man in River Bend and he hated lawbreakers. He was still smarting over that incident when the sheriff had shoved him backwards off the sidewalk. 'You want for me and one or two reliable citizens to ride out and investigate?' he asked.

'Might be a good idea,' Frederick Yango replied.

'What's happened to the sheriff, anyway?' Brig asked him. 'He's the lawman around here. Marshal Livermore too. They should be here to keep order and guard the town. That's what we elected them for, isn't it?'

Just at that moment another prominent citizen who had been waiting to welcome the gold turned to interrupt them. 'Why look!' he shouted. 'That's the stage coming right now.'

They stepped out on to Main Street and shaded their eyes to see the approaching coach.

'Why look!' Brig said, 'they got riders alongside. Five of them.'

'Yes,' Frederick Yango agreed, 'but it don't look right, does it? That's supposed to be a six horse team but, unless

123

my eyes are playing me up, I see only five.'

'I smell a big rat,' Brig Bailey said and he drew the Colt revolver from his belt.

'Looks like big trouble,' the other man added.

Frederick Yango was having difficulty putting his thoughts together. Why should there be an escort of five riders and why was one of the horses missing? 'I don't get this,' he said.

When it came to violence Brig Bailey always liked to think he was ahead of the game. So he held out his revolver and got ready for action. And it came sooner than he expected.

'Don't stop!' Wesley Carradine shouted at Sam Holtby. 'Keep right on past the depot.'

Stubbs Smith had a gun at Holtby's head, so the driver didn't have much choice.

'Where do I stop?' he shouted.

'Keep right on,' Wesley Carradine said. 'You stop if I don't tell you, you're a dead man.'

The stage careered on past the depot and the citizens waiting for it stared in amazement as it rushed by. Brig Bailey was the only one holding a gun. So Finley Finn fired a shot in his direction. The bullet took Bailey's hat right off his head and sent it flying on to the sidewalk. Bailey staggered back and almost fell. Another humiliation! But nobody laughed. They were all far too afraid for their skins.

'What the hell do they think they're doing?' Frederick Yango yelled.

'Stop right here!' Wesley Carradine said.

Sam Holtby bawled at the team and the rig came to a shuddering standstill right outside the River Bend Hotel just as a bunch of men were crowding out. A little way further down Main Street Solomon Seal had got up from his rocking-chair.

'What in tarnation's going on here?' he said just as the bouncer from The Big Gaming House stepped out on to the sidewalk. The bouncer was strapping on a gunbelt; he had been looking out down Main Street and he had an eye for trouble.

Finley Finn was still on his horse and he jigged it round for a better look at the proceedings. 'We got a problem here!' he shouted in Wesley Carradine's direction.

The men spilling out from the River Bend Hotel started dispersing in every direction like a flock of terrified hens.

The bouncer drew his gun from his gun holster and darted across Main Street surprisingly quickly for such a big man.

Stubbs Smith had his gun to Sam Holtby's head but he swung round and threw a shot in the big man's direction. The big man dodged behind a water barrel and fired a shot at Stubbs Smith.

'What the hell!' Solomon Seal roared as he dived for cover.

Colt Parry was milling around on his horse, kicking up the dust, and Jim Stacy was wheeling round, not sure what he should do.

'Get down from that rig!' Wesley Carradine shouted at Sam Holtby. 'Get down and haul out that gold!'

Sam Holtby felt like a sitting duck up there and he was only too eager to oblige. So he leaped down from the driving seat on to the sidewalk next to the River Bend Hotel. Now the horses were well and truly spooked. They pranced about, foaming at the mouth, and before anyone could take control they bolted and made off at speed down

Main Street. Stubbs Smith grabbed at the reins and attempted to take control but it was too late – nobody could have controlled those panicked horses.

Solomon Seal and the big bouncer peered out in amazement as the coach stampeded past them and roared on to the other end of the town.

Sam Holtby had barely got his hands to the box of bullion before he was hurled back on to the sidewalk where he rolled over and lay still.

Colt Parry and Jim Stacy were still on their horses and Wesley Carradine and Finley Finn were on the sidewalk.

'What in hell's name do we do now?' Finley Finn shouted.

'Only one thing we can do,' Wesley Carradine said, as he backed up to the entrance of the hotel.

At that moment the bouncer popped out from behind the water barrel on the other side of the street and fired off a round which hit Colt Parry's horse in the neck. The horse screamed and fell with its legs kicking out right in the middle of Main Street. Colt Parry had managed to leap free just in time and, as the bouncer came forward for another shot, Parry loosed one off in his direction. The bouncer jumped back and dropped his revolver. And Colt Parry ran for the entrance of the River Bend Hotel.

Just in time too; Brig Bailey was leaning on a post steadying his aim when Jim Stacy threw one at him. The bullet sent a shower of wood-shavings down on Brig Bailey's head and he retreated rapidly round the corner of a building to get his breath back.

Standing with his back to the wall, Wesley Carradine looked to his right and saw a group of men spreading out across Main Street and some of them were carrying Winchesters.

And beyond them he saw two figures on horseback riding hell for leather towards them.

'Damn me, if I'm not mistaken that's the sheriff!' he said. 'And that guy with him is Pete Pollinger, unless I'm a jackass.'

'You and me both,' Finley Finn laughed. 'The gold's on the coach. The law is on its way. What do we do now, for God's sake?'

'What we do is what we have to do,' Wesley Carradine said grimly. 'Either we mount up and ride out of town or we take ourselves into the hotel and take cover there.'

Colt Parry and Jim Stacy seemed to think that was a good idea. Jim was limping into the hotel and Colt Parry was dismounting by the hitching rail.

Wesley Carradine and Finley Finn stood one on each side of the entrance to the hotel and then all four of the bunch had retreated inside.

CHAPTER NINE

When Steve Carrington and Pete Pollinger rode into town they heard the shooting and saw men assembled outside the Wells Fargo office. Frederick Yango was signalling frantically for them to stop.

'My God, I'm glad you're here, Sheriff!' he shouted in panic. 'Those gunmen rode right into town with the coach and the bullion and now they've gone right through. Leastways, the coach has gone but the gunmen are still up there at the hotel. Looks like they aim to hole up there.'

At that moment, Brig Bailey darted down Main Street towards them and he was waving his arms like a windmill. 'There's four of them in there,' he shouted. 'I took a couple of shots at them but I couldn't bring them down.'

Steve and Pete dismounted. Pete was looking even more yellow than usual and he was coughing into a rag.

'What are we going to do?' the short-sighted Fargo agent cried.

'What we're going to do is we assess the situation and make a decision,' Steve said. He was thinking about Maria in the hotel with those desperate hombres. Pete was leaning against a post, checking his guns. If it came to a shoot-out he was the best man to have around as long as he could stand up and fire his gun.

Steve looked down Main Street and saw the bouncer moving towards them with his left hand clasping his shoulder. 'Took one in the shoulder,' he said. 'What are we gonna do?'

'I'm going to ask you boys to keep as calm as you can while I walk down Main Street and find out what those monkeys want.'

'Only one thing they want,' Frederick Yango said. 'They want the gold.'

'We'll see about that,' Steve said.

Pete Pollinger had partly recovered. He stood against the post with his Colt revolver in his hand, looking down Main Street towards the River Bend Hotel no more than three hundred feet further on.

Steve crossed the street and stepped onto the wooden sidewalk on the other side, and Pete Pollinger followed him. Brig Bailey was a few yards behind Pete.

Steve paused and looked at Bailey. 'I don't want any happy gunslinging here,' he said. 'We do this with sense and I do the talking. You understand?'

'What about those people inside the hotel?' Brig Bailey objected. 'What about Maria herself?'

Steve gave him a level look. 'I'm thinking about Maria more than anything,' he said. 'And you don't do a thing unless I say so.'

He walked on under the ramada until he was opposite the River Bend Hotel.

There were very few customers in the hotel. Most of them had scattered when the gunmen arrived. Others had disappeared through the back entrance and run off. Sam, the piano player, who had decided to stay, was just getting up from his piano seat.

When she realized what was happening Maria told the girl helpers to vamoose with the customers through the back exit. Then she stood behind the counter with her hand on the Sharp's rifle she kept there in case of trouble.

When Wesley Carradine came into the restaurant holding his revolver he saw a somewhat stately woman standing behind the counter.

'How can I help you?' Maria asked him with surprising calmness.

'You can help me by coming out from behind that counter,' Carradine said. He turned to Sam, the piano player, 'And you can sit right down again and get ready to play. I've always been partial to a little music. We might even have a dance.'

Finley Finn chuckled but he didn't sound particularly amused. He had pulled down the bandanna that was covering his lower face and Colt Parry and Jim Stacy had done the same.

'I'd like a beer if you have one,' Colt Parry said, giving Maria a shifty look.

'Will that be one beer or four?' Maria asked. 'You all look as though you could use a drink,' she added.

Wesley Carradine pulled down the bandanna covering his face, figuring concealment was no longer necessary.

Maria poured the beers and looked directly at Jim Stacy. 'Didn't I see you around town quite recently?'

Jim Stacy didn't know how to reply. His sense of humour was somewhat restricted. And Colt Parry scowled and took a quick draw on his beer.

Finley Finn swung away and looked out of the window and across the street. 'I see the sheriff and that Pete Pollinger,' he said.

130

'Pete Pollinger!' Wesley Carradine said. 'This is just the chance I need to kill that blood sucking rat!'

'What do we do now?' Colt Parry asked them. 'We could step outside and shoot them down or we could go out the back way and chance our luck.'

Finley Finn ground his teeth. 'I ain't leaving River Bend without that gold!' he declared.

Wesley was looking out of the window. 'Play our cards right we could win every way,' he said. 'You get the gold. I get Pete Pollinger. And we get to burning the whole town down to ashes.'

Maria and Sam looked at Wesley Carradine, speechless with horror.

'How come?' Finley Finn said.

'How do we play this?' Pete Pollinger asked his old army buddy.

'We talk the talk,' Steve replied.

'How do you talk to a man like Wesley Carradine?' Pete asked.

'Talk the talk is better than shoot the shoot,' Steve said. 'You should know that, Pete.'

'Did that bullet shoot out half your brains?' Pete asked in astonishment.

'If it did, I'm thinking with the other half,' Steve replied. 'Now you boys keep under cover here while I talk the talk.'

He stepped out on to Main Street and looked across at the hotel. He could see faces at the window and he could have taken a shot at them, but he was also exposed himself and he was thinking about Maria. How would he play this? He hadn't yet made up his mind. Then he cleared his throat and spoke up.

'Hello there, Wesley Carradine. I'm here to talk. Why

don't you just step outside and we can talk like two polite gents, man to man.'

'What a damned fool thing to say,' Brig Bailey muttered to Pete Pollinger.

Pete didn't reply. He watched as someone framed himself in the doorway of the hotel. It was difficult to make out who it might be, but he figured it was Wesley Carradine.

'What's the deal?' the voice came back.

Steve was leaning slightly forward towards the hotel across the street as though he was trying to pick up a faint sound. 'I don't think we have a deal here yet,' he said. 'It's just you and me having a polite chat.'

The man in the hotel doorway gave a low rumble of laughter. 'A polite chat about what?'

'Could be about how you're gonna get out of the hotel without any kind of bloodshed.'

There was a moment's silence and then someone threw open a window on the second floor. 'There ain't gonna be no bloodshed if you do as you're bid,' a voice shouted from the window.'

'That's Finley Finn,' Pete Pollinger said to Brig Bailey. 'You can't make deals with an *hombre* like that.'

Finley Finn had got himself into what he thought was a commanding position. He could see both ways along the street. His only problem was that he couldn't see what was happening under the shade of the ramada opposite.

Then Steve Carrington spoke again. 'Maybe you should spell out what you want from this,' he said.

The man in the doorway of the hotel shifted slightly. That's a foolish move, Steve thought. One in the doorway and one upstairs. So they can't be speaking with one voice.

It was Wesley Carradine who spoke again. 'I'll tell you what we want, Sheriff. We want the gold and Pete Pollinger.

I see he's right behind you there. You ask him to throw down his gun and walk across the street. Then you get the gold and load it on a buck-board. So we can ride out of town and everyone will be happy.'

'What happens if we don't agree?' Pete Pollinger called out from behind Steve.

'Well, in that case,' the man in the window said, 'the life of the lady who owns this establishment might be in considerable danger.'

'What you do is Pollinger delivers the gold and we deliver the lady. That's the deal,' Wesley Carradine called out.

'That isn't going to be easy,' Steve said. 'You must know what happened. The horses spooked and the stage rolled out of town with the gold.'

There was a pause.

'Well, that's the deal. You get that gold and bring it back here. You load it on a buckboard and we ride out of town.'

'That's a damned fool of a deal,' Pete muttered. He looked down to the right but the stage was out of sight. It might be half way to Mexico by now.

In fact Stubbs Smith had got control of the horses and hauled the coach to a standstill. He looked back along the trail towards the last buildings of the town. The horses were exhausted and needed to rest up and be fed and watered. There was no chance of pushing them on even if he wanted to. But did he want to?

He sat in the driving seat and considered his position. And then he heard voices. Two men came, driving horses from further along the trail. When they saw the rig standing idle they shook their heads and stared at Stubbs Smith.

'Those horses look plumb tuckered out,' the older man said. 'Where you riding to? This ways is to South Fork. I ain't never seen Fargo coaches this far out of town.'

The younger man who wasn't much more than a pimpled youth looked at the coach team. 'You had trouble, mister? Looks like you lost one of your team.'

'Did you run into trouble?' the older man asked suspiciously, eyeing the gun holster on Stubbs Smith's hip.

'Back there in town,' Stubbs Smith lied. 'A bunch of *hombres* tried to hold up the coach but I managed to break away.'

'That takes a deal of grit,' the older man said. 'Why don't you water those poor critters before they drop dead from thirst on you?'

'There's a pool just off the trail here,' the youth said. He had dismounted and was already making himself useful, unhitching the team and leading them off the trail to the pool.

'I need a buggy,' Stubbs Smith said. 'You know where I could find a buggy?'

The older man gave him a puzzled look. 'What you need a buggy fer, mister?'

'I got to get my cargo on, that's why.'

'You got cargo,' the older man said. 'What cargo would that be?' He sidled closer and ducked down to look inside the coach. When he turned to look at Stubbs Smith, he saw Stubbs was pointing a Colt .45 at him.

Wesley Carradine disappeared inside the hotel and Finley Finn stood behind the window above. Steve Carrington heard voices raised in the hotel, angry voices he could hear from across Main Street.

Keep calm, he said to himself; don't let your emotions run wild.

Finley Finn leaned forward a little. 'The big man's

134

getting mad,' he said. 'You know Wes? He can run awful wild when he's mad. People can get killed.'

Steve looked up at the face in the window and knew he could have shot it right between the eyes, but what good would that do?

Pete was standing beside him. 'Listen,' he said. 'I'm going to throw down my gun and go right over there and give myself up.'

Steve had turned to him. 'And what would that do, Pete? Use your head. You go over there, they'll have two hostages instead of one.'

Pete thought for a moment. 'What if I offer myself in exchange for Maria? They might buy that.'

Then two things happened almost simultaneously. From further down the trail where the coach had disappeared there came the sound of a shot. And then, immediately afterwards, there came a surge of men from outside the Wells Fargo depot. Local people, some of them carrying shot guns, some carrying old fashioned rifles, and some toting pitchforks and axes. And among them, Steve saw the bald head of Eleazer Stebbins and the somewhat lean form of Mayor Shapley.

Finley Finn ducked inside the hotel and ran down the window.

The crowd surged on until it came to the River Bend Hotel.

Mayor Shapley strode up to Steve with a long barrelled Colt in his hand. 'So they're in there!' he shouted.

Steve nodded briefly. 'They're in there and they're holding Maria hostage,' he said.

'What about the gold? Have they got the gold?'

For the first time Steve felt his patience was about to snap. 'The gold be damned!' he said. 'We're talking about people's lives here.'

Mayor Shapley bristled up. 'As mayor of this town, I'm taking charge,' he said. 'I've sent armed men round to the back of the hotel to cut them off. Then we smoke them out.'

Several men in the crowd raised a cheer.

'Listen, Mayor, you might be taking charge, but there are lives at stake here. You rush into things innocent blood will be shed.'

'Tell you what you can do,' Pete suddenly piped up. 'If you want that gold so bad you can walk right out of town in the direction of the South Fork. That's where the coach is and that's where the gold is.'

Shapley looked at Pete in distrust for a moment and then changed his mind. 'Come on, boys,' he said with a sweep of his arm. 'The coach went this way. We got to save that gold before those hombres get their hands on it.' And he rushed off towards the end of town, followed by a crowd of eager followers.

'Thank you, Pete,' Steve said. 'I think you went some way to saving the day there, buddy.'

Next moment he was confronted by a frantic Eleazer Stebbins. 'What can I do to help?' Stebbins shouted. 'Give me a gun so I can go in there!' The sight of a bald youth who looked like a monk offering to storm into the hotel and shoot the gunmen caused everyone to gasp in astonishment.

'Well, Eleazer,' Steve advised, 'I think you should leave this to the law. Father Sylvester will need you. So you'd better not let him down.'

Stubbs Smith turned from the bleeding man towards the advancing crowd. He saw Mayor Shapley coming towards him, levelling a gun with six or seven other men, some of them prominent citizens and others just outraged citizens.

The older horse herder was lying on the ground gasping and bleeding profusely and the spooked horses were prancing and rearing and galloping away down the trail. The younger herder was standing on the edge of the trail, not knowing whether to flee or drop down behind an acacia bush.

'Drop that gun!' Shapley commanded. 'Drop that gun and put your hands up!'

Stubbs Smith wasn't about to drop anything. He swung round and fired a shot at the mayor. The bullet caught Shapley right below the shoulder and he fell back like a log.

The advancing crowd gasped with horror and made as if to back off, but one of the younger men hurled an axe in Stubbs Smith's direction. Stubbs Smith tried to duck but he was an instant too late. The axe blade caught him right in the middle of the forehead and he dropped back like a stone with blood spurting from a split in his skull.

Maria was standing in front of the bar of the hotel and Wesley Carradine was holding a gun to her head. She could hear the crowd shouting outside in the street and she knew that her life was right on the edge. In the next minute or two she might die. They say when you drown your whole life flashes before you in a series of pictures, but Maria saw no pictures; she just wondered what it would be like when Wesley Carradine pulled the trigger. Would she feel the bullet thud into her brain? Would it just be darkness in which she wouldn't even remember having lived? She felt no panic; just a kind of deep sadness that life was about to slip away from her.

Then Finley Finn came into the bar room carrying a

hand gun and a Winchester. 'The whole town is beginning to roar, Wes. I don't know quite what we do. That sheriff talks as if he knows a whole lot of things we don't know.'

'Like what?' Wesley Carradine said.

'And I've just seen a bunch of men going on past down Main Street in the direction the stage went with the gold.'

Colt Parry had been investigating a possible escape route at the back. 'They got men out there just waiting to shoot us down,' he said with a note of panic.

'No need to worry about that,' Jim Stacy replied. 'They ain't gonna shoot us down as long as we got our guns on this woman and the piano player.'

Sam was still sitting on the piano stool wondering what he could do. He was a highly sensitive man and his hands were shaking so much he knew he wouldn't be able to play a single chord.

Wesley Carradine took the gun from Maria's head and started pacing up and down. When he glanced out of the window he could see Steve Carrington and Pete Pollinger standing on Main Street with Brig Bailey and Eleazer Stebbins. Stebbins was nothing more than a spot-faced kid but the others were tooled up and ready for a fight. Except that Pete Pollinger was actually smoking a quirly. The sight of that quirly sent the fire of hate running right through Carradine's soul. 'I could shoot that bastard to hell right where he stands!' he muttered. 'I could go to the front porch and shoot that thing right out of his mouth and scatter his brains.'

'Steady there,' Finley Finn warned him. 'Use that high mind of yours. You said we could have the gold and your revenge as well. And you want to burn the whole place down too.'

Wesley Carradine continued pacing back and forth.

138

'Something tells me the gold is out of reach,' he said.

'That gold can't be far,' Jim Stacy suggested. 'How about if we use the woman to bargain for the gold. What we do is demand a buggy with the gold on board. Then we take the woman and this piano tickler hostage and we ride right out of town.'

'I don't think that will work,' Wesley Carradine said. 'It sounds a mite too easy.'

Then Maria spoke up. 'Why don't you boys realize you aren't going anywhere? If you'd care to sit down and take a drink. Put your guns on the floor and relax. Then we can organize some kind of solution to this problem?'

Wesley Carradine and Finley Finn stared at one another aghast. 'Are you in your right mind, woman?' Finley Finn said.

'Probably not,' she said. 'But it's the only way you're going to avoid getting yourselves killed.'

Wesley Carradine and Finley Finn looked at one another again. Could they believe what they were hearing?

Jim Stacy could see the point. Which was they were never going to get out of this damned hotel alive. 'I think we should forget about the gold,' he said. 'What we do is to get horses and take the woman out of town with us and ride for the border. That's the best thing we can do.'

On the other side of Main Street Steve checked his watch and realized the sun was getting quite low in the sky. It would soon be dark and they were getting nowhere at all. Not only that; when he looked to the west he saw a sizeable cloud building up on the jagged horizon.

'Steve, there's going to be the mother of all storms,' Pete said beside him, 'and that's not gonna improve the situation. Those skookums in there will be nice and cosy and we'll be wet to our toes. They've got plenty of supplies in there and they can last out for more than a month if necessary.'

Brig Bailey said, 'That's no big problem. I can send down to Little Nell's place to arrange dinner and we can go down there in shifts.'

'I don't want no dinner,' Eleazer Stebbins said. 'Not till we smoke those gunmen out of there. You give me a gun and I'll go in right now.'

Now there was a rattling and clinking as the stage started back along Main Street with Mayor Stapley leading the way triumphantly. 'We got the gold!' he shouted as he rode up. 'There's one man severely wounded and one of those gunmen with his head split open and dead. You making any progress here, Sheriff?'

'We're waiting, Mr Mayor,' Steve called back.

The stage trundled by with the team being led by several local men, none of whom cared to perch on the driver's seat, partly because Stubbs Smith was dead and partly because they didn't want to risk being shot down from inside the hotel.

Under cover of the passing coach, Pete Pollinger made a sudden move. He ducked down and crossed the street at a fast sprint. When the coach had passed, Steve saw him flattening himself against the wall of the building next to the hotel.

'What in hell's name does he think he's doing?' Steve asked himself.

The next moment the door of the hotel opened and Maria staggered out in front of Wesley Carradine who had a gun at her head.

'Talk to the man, pretty lady,' Wesley Carradine ordered. 'Tell him what he must do.'

140

Maria stood as tall as she could but Steve could see she was fighting hard to keep her composure.

'Steve,' she said with a tremor in her voice. 'I'm OK but I'm like to die if you don't get a buggy with the gold on board.'

'That's the deal,' Wesley Carradine echoed. 'We get the gold and we ride out of town and everybody's going to be happy.'

'That's damned right,' Finley Finn said from behind him.

'Keep talking,' Steve said to himself. He stood with his legs apart and his hands held out wide as he tried to assess the situation. He could feel Brig Bailey breathing fire on his right and Eleazer Stebbins anxious to prove himself on his left and he could see Pete flattened against the doorway across the street next to the hotel.

He looked straight into Maria's eyes and saw some kind of signal it was difficult to read, a kind of resolve mingled with terror.

All round him the air seemed as taut as a bowstring just before an arrow is fired.

Such moments can last no more than a second but that second seems to stretch to infinity. You don't think much but you have all the time in the world.

Then two things happened. Over to the west there was a sudden crack of thunder and, crouching in the doorway, Pete suddenly started to cough. He couldn't help himself. It was enough to distract Wesley Carradine's attention, just briefly but long enough.

Maria hurled herself right off the sidewalk and on to Main Street. In that instant Steve realized what she had been signalling to him and he acted before he had time to think about it. He pulled his gun and fired.

Wesley Carradine fired a split second later, but a split second too late. The glass in a window behind Steve shattered and Carradine pitched back into the doorway of the hotel.

Pete was still coughing when he fired his gun at Finley Finn. Finley Finn fired off a shot and then staggered towards Pete, clawing at him with his left hand and thumbing his gun with his right. Then both fired again and both fell.

Steve's main concern was for Maria. He ran forward and stooped beside her. She looked up at him in amazement. 'Protect yourself!' she cried.

Steve lurched forward with his gun and saw Wesley Carradine writhing on his back in the doorway of the hotel and two bodies lying a few feet apart to his right.

Almost immediately Brig Bailey was beside him, looking down at Finley Finn. Finley Finn tried to raise his gun but his strength had drained away. Something rattled in his throat and he fell back, dead.

Steve knelt beside Wesley Carradine and took his weapon. Carradine opened his eyes and tried to smile.

The next instant Father Sylvester was kneeling beside Carradine, speaking in a clear cool tone the last rites of the dying.

Steve moved to Pete and knelt beside him. 'You hit bad?' he said.

With some help from Brig Bailey, Pete had now managed to prop himself up against the door jam and he was coughing up blood and crying out in agony. 'I been hit,' he managed to say, 'but I think I might be OK.'

The next moment Doc MacFadden was there. He pronounced Finley Finn dead and knelt down beside Pete Pollinger. 'You've got a bullet in your shoulder,' he said. 'I'll need to get you back to my place.'

Brig Bailey stood beside Pete and put his hand on his shoulder. 'That was damned fine shooting,' he said.

Steve took a deep breath. 'That wasn't damned fine shooting.' he said. 'That was a shot I couldn't miss. I guess I need a drink.'

Maria was on her feet again, but now she was crying. Steve helped her to the edge of the sidewalk and she sat and put her head in her hands and cried with relief. 'Thank God!' she said. 'Thank God.'

As they carried Pete away to the doctor's surgery on a stretcher they heard more shots from behind the hotel.

'That must be Colt Parry and Jim Stacy trying to break away,' Steve said.

'No more bloodshed,' Father Sylvester said. 'There's been enough blood spilled this day.'

When they went into the hotel lobby there was nobody in view. As Steve was walking right through the bar room a pale face peered over the bar and looked at him. It was Sam, the piano player.

'What's happening?' Sam gasped. He looked like a circus clown with a chalk white face.

'It's OK, Sam. You can come out now,' Steve told him.

'Is Maria safe?' the clown-like face asked.

'Maria's OK,' Steve assured him. 'What happened to the other two skookums?'

Sam came out from behind the bar. 'I think they went through the back way when the shooting started.'

Steve continued on to the back entrance and found the door wide open. Half a dozen men and youths were crowding round the form of a man lying on the ground. As Steve approached they drew back in wonderment. 'They done killed Cal Warrender!' one of the men said.

Steve looked down at the dead man and shook his head. 'Where did they go?'

'They grabbed horses and rode away that way!' the man said, pointing to his right.

An older man tried to explain. 'We tried to stop them but those bastards just let off their guns. Lucky no one else was killed.'

Cal Warrender, the dead man, had been what some might call a good and upright citizen. When someone needed help he was always the first to step forward and this was his reward. He was lying on his back with his eyes wide open in amazement.

They carried him down to the funeral director's by a back way. Nobody wanted to see him lying beside those dead killers.

The good and the bad, it makes no difference; we all go the same way, Steve thought.

'You think we should ride out after those two killers, Sheriff?' someone asked.

'Soon enough, soon enough,' Steve said. 'One thing's for certain, they won't come back here in a hurry.'

CHAPTER TEN

The funeral director had never been so busy. He didn't have enough coffins in stock so he was working all out, fashioning caskets. But there was no democracy in death so the caskets he made for the righteous were a lot fancier than those he made for the killers. The righteous like Jake Brekenville and John Gullimore, and especially Cal Warrender, had fancy brass handles and screws fitted to them. The killers had pine handles and the lids of their coffins were nailed down, but only after they were put on display for several hours outside the funeral parlour. That was Mayor Shapley's decision. He looked down at those dead faces with Federal Marshal Livermore and said proudly, 'Marshal, I think we did a good job there.'

Marshal Livermore stood with his hand on his chest above his coat where it buttoned up looking like the Emperor Napoleon with a cigar in the corner of his mouth. 'We certainly cleared the town of those villainous men,' he boasted. 'And we got that guy who molested the good fathers in custody too,' he said, referring to Chuck Cherokee who was now in the town jail waiting for the

145

district judge to arrive.

Steve also looked down at those dead faces and his reaction was somewhat different. Even a villain can look peaceful in death. When the bullet had struck Wesley Carradine he had probably been surprised and now he seemed to be smiling secretly to himself as though he had seen something that none of the living had been permitted to glimpse. On the other hand, Finley Finn's features were creased in wonder as though he couldn't quite believe Pete Pollinger had got the drop on him.

Steve took off his hat and waved a fly away from Finley Finn's face. That fly's more alive than Finn can ever be now, he thought. Funny how small a man can look when the life's gone out of him.

'It's time they took these bodies into the shade,' someone said from beside him. He turned and saw Father Sylvester looking down at those dead faces. With him were two monks and the youth Eleazer Stebbins. Stebbins looked kind of yellow in the gills.

Steve went through to the funeral director's workshop and saw the funeral director and his young assistant busy putting together pine coffins. 'I think you should bring those corpses into the shade and nail down the lids,' he said to the funeral director.

The funeral director straightened up with his hand pressed against his back to ease his back ache 'I agree with you, Sheriff. It's just that the mayor thought it would be good for the folk of River Bend to see what happens when you take it into your head to steal and kill around here.' He was smiling with a faint air of professional pride.

'Well, I think the mayor has made his point,' Steve said. 'Those sad corpses are starting to stink and the good citizens of River Bend aren't going to like that much, are they?'

146

The funeral director nodded officiously. 'Just what I think, Sheriff. I'll see about it directly.'

'Directly is now,' Steve said.

'Yessir,' the funeral director said.

Outside, a considerable crowd had gathered and Father Sylvester and the monks were standing by the coffins with their heads bowed as though in prayer.

'Pray for the living, not for the dead,' someone shouted angrily.

The funeral director emerged with his assistant and the monks helped them to carry the coffins into the premises.

Eleazer Stebbins stood on his own, still somewhat yellow in the gills. Steve put his hand on the boy's shoulder. 'Why don't you just sit in the shade for a while,' he said.

Stebbins shook his head. 'I'm gonna be all right,' he said. 'I just didn't like looking at those dead faces. It gives me the creeps.'

'The shows over,' Steve said to the people. 'There's plenty to do in this town. So why don't you just go about your business?'

Someone chuckled. Steve had a way of defusing trouble: he made people laugh. As the people drifted away to their shops, businesses and bordellos, Steve and Eleazer Stebbins sat on a bench on the sidewalk.

'You done could have shot me like one of them,' Stebbins said. 'That time I tried for a hold-up.'

'I guess I could if I had to,' Steve admitted, 'but luckily I didn't have to.'

'That Brig Bailey would have had me swinging by the neck from one of those rafters too.'

'Well, that's true as well,' Steve said. 'It just means you're a lucky Jim.'

147

'It was partly through you and that judge that I wound up with Father Sylvester.'

'Father Sylvester's a good man,' Steve said. He looked at the kid from the corner of his eye. 'Aren't you glad I didn't give you a gun when those two killers came to the door?'

Eleazer Stebbins creased his young brows. 'I thought it was payback time for the good you done me but I'm right glad you didn't give me that gun.'

'What are you going to do now?' Steve asked him.

'Oh, I aim to stay with the Fathers,' he said with surprising decisiveness. 'I think they're the nearest thing I got to a proper family.'

Steve rose from the bench and patted the boy on the shoulder as Father Sylvester and the monks emerged from the funeral parlour. Father Sylvester looked down at the boy. 'We think it's time to leave now, Eleazer.'

Eleazer sprang up eagerly. 'I'm with you, Father,' he said. 'Thanks, Steve, thanks.' He seized Steve's hand and started to pump it.

'We'll be back for the funerals,' Father Sylvester said to Steve.

'Thank you,' Steve said.

Steve walked over to Doc MacFadden's surgery. 'How's the patient?' he asked the doc.

Doctor MacFadden scowled. 'He's dying,' he said.

Steve stared at him. 'You mean like dying right now?'

'No, not right now, but he has an incurable consumption and a bullet wound in the shoulder doesn't help either. By the natural turn of events he should be in the ground already, but he has remarkable determination. I don't think I've ever encountered a man with such a zest for life.'

'Pete was always like that,' Steve said. 'He saved my life on more than one occasion during the war when we were in the army together. If it wasn't for Pete I wouldn't be here talking to you like this.'

Doc MacFadden took Steve by the arm. 'I have to tell you something, Steve.' MacFadden looked at the door as if to make sure that no one was listening. 'Last night your friend had an attack of some kind that I found very puzzling. When I heard him raving I looked in and saw him walking round the room, muttering to himself. He had his eyes wide open and he was talking to himself quite loudly. Somnambulism, you know, or sleepwalking. It happens when a man or woman is deeply troubled.'

'Maybe I could look in and see him,' Steve said.

The doc looked thoughtful. 'You can see him but try to keep him calm. He needs to rest.'

Steve found Pete out of bed and trying to dress himself though he was hampered by having his left arm in a sling and his shoulder bound up tight with bandages.

'Good to see you, buddy,' he said. 'I got to get out of here. That doc is a really caring *hombre*, but he makes me feel like death warmed up. Help me to get my rags on. I've got things to do.'

As Steve helped his old army comrade to dress he felt his frail bones and realized he'd dropped down to a mere shadow of his former self. 'If you must leave you've got to come down to the hotel. Maria has given me strict instructions to take you there so you can feed up and get fat again.'

'Just like the golden goose.' Pete tried to laugh and his laugh turned into a prolonged coughing fit.

Doc MacFadden was framed in the doorway. He shook his head sadly but fatalistically. 'So you've decided to discharge yourself.'

149

'Can't overstay my welcome,' Pete said. 'Got things to do in the great wide world out there and I have to do them while there's still breath in my body.'

'So where will you go?' the doctor asked him.

Pete stood up and almost looked like his earlier self apart from the shoulder binding and the sling. 'Well, sir, first I have to thank you for patching me up real good. Then I'm going to walk up to the River Bend Hotel to rest up for a day. I might even break the rules and drink a pint of rye whiskey and smoke a cigar or two. I know that would be detrimental to my health but what the hell, anyway. At least I shall die happy.'

Doc MacFadden regarded him philosophically. 'Well, you're probably right at that,' he said.

Pete held up his free hand. 'But before the dark angel comes swooping out of the clouds, I have one more thing to do.'

'Indeed, you do,' Doc MacFadden agreed. 'You could offer up a prayer and make peace with whatever God you believe in.'

'Well,' Pete said, 'I'm not sure that guy up yonder believes in me. But I am sure about one thing: I got a certain little hoard of money stashed away and I want to clear it before I die.'

Steve and Pete walked down Main Street together until they arrived at the River Bend Hotel. Maria and some of her staff were waiting to receive them. The two men felt like royalty, the way they were treated.

Maria had recovered from the traumas of the shootout and had got herself back into some kind of normality but nobody can come out of an experience like that without changing.

'I've been waiting for you,' she said to Pete. 'I've put you in the best room. It's not quite the royal suite but it's the best River Bend can offer.'

Pete sat down on a chair to catch his breath. 'You didn't need to put yourself to so much trouble,' he said. 'I just want to sit out on the back for a while, smoking cigars and drinking if my cough will allow me to. I could just sit in a rocking-chair out there and admire the view some. Tomorrow Steve and me have travel plans.'

'What plans would those be?' Steve asked him.

'Those plans are the pot of gold at the end of the rainbow,' Pete said. 'Those dollars Wesley Carradine thought I stole from him which in fact was just the cream of the milk he stole from other people – mostly rich folk who, in turn, stole from the poor folk.'

It was a fine warm day and the earlier storm had washed away most of the traces of the gunfight. They took Pete out to sit in the rocking-chair he had dreamed about and gave him a big fat cigar and a tall glass of rye and he sat sipping the rye and smoking until the sun started to dip towards the horizon.

Maria and Steve sat across a table in the hotel lobby and looked at one another. Sam had come in with his wife and they began to play a quiet duet together.

'I didn't know Sam's wife played piano,' Steve said.

'Oh, she plays,' Maria said. 'She plays real good. They met in some music school back east. Sam wanted to be a real class performer. But he ended up here.' She looked across at the pair playing the piano so happily together. 'She thought she was going to lose him,' she said wistfully. 'But thank God he survived.'

Steve sat at the table and looked across at Maria. She

151

was smiling.

'Thank you,' she said.

'Thank you for what?'

'Thank you for saving me. Without your quick thinking I'd have died.'

Steve shook his head. 'Without your quick thinking we might have both died.'

They sat looking at one another.

'You want to know something,' he said. 'We make a very good partnership.'

'What are we going to do about that?' she asked him.

'I think we should get married,' he said.

She stretched out her hand across the table and he took it in both of his and carried it to his lips and kissed it.

Next morning come sun-up Pete had somehow got himself out of bed. Sitting at the table at breakfast he was still slightly drunk, but he seemed frail but happy. His eyes were deep in their sockets but they gleamed with a lust for life.

'Did they saddle up my horse?' he asked Steve.

'The horses are waiting on us,' Steve said. He had had both horses groomed and ready. 'You think you should go?'

'Only thing to stop me is that black angel I was talking about and I'm hoping he's gonna be gentle when he comes.'

It felt like the last supper to Steve though he didn't know why.

Pete looked first left and then right along Main Street. 'I wonder what will happen to that Chuck Cherokee, languishing there in your gaol?'

'Maybe they'll hang him,' Steve said.

'What about those two who got away? They're still out

there somewhere looking for revenge.'

Steve tipped his hat back on his head. 'I think we can leave that to Marshal Livermore,' he said with a smile.

They rode back along the trail towards High Rock, passing the place where the Wells Fargo coach with the bullion had been held up. The storm had washed out all signs of the hold up and now the sun was hot in the sky.

'Where are you taking me?' Steve asked.

Pete gave a low laugh; he was reserving his energy. 'Well, one thing's for sure,' he said. 'I ain't taking you back to the County Penitentiary and that's a certainty.'

They rode up through the chaparral and then among the creosote bushes with their yellow flowers towards higher ground.

'Good for the rheumatics, so they tell me,' Pete said as they rode among the creosote bushes. 'The Mexicans believe it cures the aches and pains if you rub it in. Do you believe that, Steve?'

'I have no opinion either way,' Steve said. 'If the Apaches told me it was so I might try it. Those guys have a lot of stored up wisdom.'

They were riding on, heel to heel, at a leisurely pace.

'I guess they don't know a way to treat the consumption, do they?' Pete asked him.

Steve shook his head. 'You'd need to ask a medicine man about that,' he said.

Pete tossed his head. 'Too late for me anyways,' he said, 'now that I'm almost face to face with that big mystery.'

They rode on in silence for a while.

'Where are you taking me, anyway?' Steve asked him.

'Well, it ain't too far from here, I can promise you, and I don't think you'll be disappointed either.'

They were now climbing steadily.

'It wouldn't be the Old Silver Mine Workings, would it?' Steve asked him.

'You mean where Wesley Carradine and his bunch were holed up?' Pete said in a teasing voice.

'The very same,' Steve said.

'Well, strange you should mention that, my old pard,' Pete replied with that strange twinkle in his eye.

Shortly afterwards, the Old Silver Workings came into view. Just a collection of dilapidated buildings, some of them almost broken away into nothing. There was just one cabin that was still inhabitable and that was the one where the two women had tried to keep house for Carradine and his bunch.

'I wonder where those two women are now?' Pete reflected.

'Oh, they're as much as likely south of the border looking for Mexican husbands,' Steve said.

They dismounted and kicked open the door of the cabin and several rats scampered away into their holes. Steve drew his gun and stepped inside. He wasn't taking any chances. Jim Stacy and Colt Parry might have come back to the place just for one night.

'What a dump!' Steve said. 'How could those two women have cooked anything on that apology for a stove?'

He poked about in the side rooms and saw old mattresses strewn about the floor.

'What a way to live! Even those dumb rats have it better.' He picked up the witch's broom Bess Woodman had used to sweep the dust off the porch. 'Well,' he said. 'Wesley Carradine must have had something, the way he kept those women.'

'You're right on that,' Pete said. 'When I had the

misfortune to ride with him, I thought he was king.'

'That didn't stop you from filching from him, did it?'

'No, it didn't stop me. I was greedy like the rest of them. And that's why he wanted to kill me.'

Steve looked at him and wondered how he could still be standing, let alone talking. 'Then, why have you brought me here?' he asked.

Pete had to pause to have another coughing fit. It lasted so long Steve thought it would never stop. Then Pete fought to get his breath back.

'Give me your arm and I'll show you,' he said at last.

Steve stood beside him and Pete took his arm. It was like leading a really old man.

They went out and along to the ruins of the old winding-mill a hundred feet away. The winding mill was so dilapidated it looked like a drunk about to collapse into the dust.

'In here,' Pete gasped. 'To the left here.'

They went inside. Pete pointed to a large slab of stone.

'Roll that to one side,' he said. 'It's heavy and I couldn't do it anymore, but you can do it, my friend. I'll just sit me down here a mite and watch.' He sat back against the wall and gasped.

Steve stooped to the rock and took a grip of it.

'Now lift and roll,' Pete instructed quietly.

Steve knelt down and with difficulty raised the stone and rolled it away. Beneath it a cavernous hole appeared.

'Reach down, reach down,' Pete said impatiently. 'You should find a leather bag down there.'

Steve reached right down and searched with his hand. There was very little light.

'It should be down there,' Pete said with feverish excitement.

Steve searched from left to right and then back again. This is crazy, he thought. But then his hand made contact with something that felt like leather.

'I think I've got it,' he said.

Pete sighed. 'Haul it up and look inside.'

Steve dragged the bag out of the cavity. It was covered with dust. He held it up for Pete to see.

'Open it, open it!' Pete gasped. 'Open it and look inside.'

Steve undid a strap and pulled back the flap.

'What do you see?'

Steve peered closer. 'I see dollar bills. Many of them.'

Pete sighed again. 'That's what you see, my friend. That's what you see.' He leaned back and slid down the wall and lay.

Steve pushed the bag aside and went to his friend.

Pete opened his eyes and tried to smile. Then he fell back and died.

'Five thousand dollars,' Steve said to Maria. 'Five thousand dollars!'

They were once again at the River Bend Hotel, staring at one another across the table.

'You brought him in across the saddle of his horse,' Maria said.

'Only thing I could do,' he said.

When he realized that Pete was dead he dragged the body out to the horse and lifted him across its back. It wasn't particularly dignified but it was the only thing he could do. As he lifted the body, he talked to Pete as though he was still alive. 'I'm sorry to do it this way, my friend, but there was no other way.'

When he rode into town leading Pete's horse with Pete's

body hanging over it, everyone came out to look. 'My God,' some said, 'has there been another shooting?'

Mayor Shapley, who was writing down figures in his office, looked up and saw Steve and the horse with the body. He had watched earlier as the two had ridden out together. So he was deeply suspicious.

Now he came out of his office and stood staring as Steve drew up outside the funeral director's office and went inside. After a few moments the funeral director came bustling outside with his assistant. The horse turned its head to watch as they lifted Pete's body down and carried it inside.

'I want the best,' Steve said to the funeral director. 'I'm going to ask Father Sylvester to take charge and do everything as it should be. Maybe with a choir too. I believe those monks can sing really well.'

'What happened?' Mayor Shapley asked. As the elected mayor he felt it was his business to know everything that happened in the town.

Steve explained that he had taken Pete up to the Old Silver Mine Workings for some reason and that poor Pete's heart had given out and he had died. Mayor Shapley wasn't altogether happy about that explanation but when Doc MacFadden examined the corpse and said he couldn't imagine how Pete Pollinger had managed to survive the ride all the way up to the Silver Workings, even the mayor was satisfied.

They gave Pete a grand funeral. Though Pete had not been a believer, at least in the orthodox sense, Father Sylvester had agreed to officiate and several of the monks had sung as Sam the pianist played the piano. There was no organ, of course. Steve wasn't a speaker but he pulled himself together and spoke naturally about his old friend Pete

Pollinger, how Pete had been his sergeant during the war and how Pete had saved his life on more than one occasion. Yes, after the war Pete had turned to crime, but he wasn't the first and he wouldn't be the last. It wasn't a long speech but it came right from the heart.

After the ceremony, Steve spoke to Father Sylvester.

'Father Sylvester,' he said. 'I want to thank you. I know my friend would have been proud. I think he was a believer in his own way though I don't know what his beliefs were exactly.'

Father Sylvester smiled. 'I don't think we should worry too much about that.'

'And there's something I need to ask you,' Steve said.

'Well, ask away,' the priest said.

Steve reached down and picked up the bag he had retrieved from under the stone. Now it was polished up really well. 'Pete and I want you to have this for the Jesuit House,' he said as he placed the bag on the table.

'What's this?' Father Sylvester asked.

'That's approximately five thousand dollars,' Steve said. 'Pete would want you to have it for the good work you do.'

Father Sylvester looked down at the bag but, if he was amazed, he didn't show it. 'Thank you,' he said. 'We will use it well.'

'Good,' Steve nodded. He felt a great load fall from his shoulders.

'One more thing,' he said.

'What is that, my son?'

'Well, just as soon as we can arrange it, Maria and me would like you to officiate at our wedding.'

Father Sylvester smiled. 'That will be a real pleasure, Steve,' he said.